Breakfast At Earl's

To two outstanding neighbors,
Katie and Eick —
    I hope you will
enjoy at least a couple of stories —

Van Pittman, August 12, 2019 !

Breakfast At Earl's

A Collection of Short Fiction and Nonfiction

Von V. Pittman

Compass Flower Press
Columbia, Missouri

Layout by Yolanda Ciolli of Compass Flower Press

Published by
Compass Flower Press
Columbia, Missouri

Library of Congress Control Number: 2019911108

ISBN 978-1-942168-69-0 Trade Paperback

The following stories have been previously published, some with altered titles:

Getting Out the Vote! / Strange Bedfellows
Well Versed, 2006 Columbia Writers' Guild

"Now and Then"
Diamonds in the Rough, 2007, Missouri State Poetry Society

"Lee Harvey Oswald: Whistle and Thump"
Well Versed, 2011; Columbia Writers' Guild

"Low Inside Heat"
Storm Country Anthology MWG, 2011; MOZark Press

"Romeo Corpen"
Deep Waters, 2012, Outrider Press.

'Tommy Hawk's Boys'
Well Versed, 2013, Columbia Writers' Guild

"Red Shirt Record"
Cuivre River Vol VII, 2013, Saturday Writers

"Yankee Station: On the Line"
Interpretations III, 2015; Columbia Art League

"Fun on Wall Street"
Well Versed, 2016; Columbia Writers' Guild

"Obstacle No. Three"
Under the Surface, Volume No. 8, 2017; Saturday Writers

"A Talk With a Stranger" and "Barnstormers Trajectory"
Eternal as a Weed, 2017; Creative Writing of Columbia;
Bridget Bufford, Editor

"A Ferret's Lot"
Boundless, 2018; Compass Flower Press
David Collins, Editor

Other stories in this collected volume may also have appeared previously in printed and/or online publications.

Dedication

My wife, Joyce Pittman is a talented and intelligent healer of fractured prose and bruised egos. Without her, I could not have sustained this project.

Table of Contents

Formal Indoctrinations
Fiction

Salty Waters
Fiction

Other Diversions

Introduction

Von Pittman has attended my writing workshops faithfully for the past fifteen years; I have written more with him than with any other person. Initially Von seemed a bit shy and self–deprecating, and it was a joy to see his confidence grow as he continued to write and participate.

In that time his baritone recitations have graced the workshop with craft, humor, and story, with smiles and snickers and an occasional booming laugh. When I told my partner Becky that Von would no longer be attending, she was pained. She always liked his writings, especially the ones about the Vietnam War. "Not hearing his voice feels like a void to me," she said. "Tell him thanks for filling up our house with your aircraft carrier stories all these years, and we will be poorer for no longer having him here."

Introduction

I have been privileged to experience many of Von's stories from inception to conclusion, and I envy his ability to tell a complete tale so concisely. He remained a bit critical of his writing and reworked his pieces tirelessly. The results of this attention to detail and craft await you: lean, finely–honed stories with extraordinary characters, ones you will never forget. This collection makes me very happy.

—Bridget Bufford
Author, *Cemetery Bird* 2011
Editor, *Eternal as a Weed* 2017

Formal Indoctrinations

From Administrivia to Creativity

We tend to think of writing produced by bureaucrats and administrative functionaries as boring, bloated, and even deadly. And that is often true. But this is a simplistic way of looking at what can be effective and even beneficial experience for writers who aspire to publish works of creative fiction and nonfiction.

In forty years of professional and academic administration, I wrote hundreds of thousands of words in the forms of objectives, goals, plans, "how-to" pieces, briefings, and other administrative works. At first glance such documents might not appear to provide a foundation for creative writing.

To the contrary, I would argue. Have you ever had to read a strategic plan for a university, a corporation, or a military unit? The drafters of these documents fill them with—nay, rely upon—what lawyers call "facts not in evidence." Indeed, organizations typically base their strategic plans on flights of fantasy most science fiction editors would summarily reject. In written descriptions of how their units work, managers romanticize to a degree that would make a Harlequin editor blush. And when codifying procedures, rules, and regulations, bureaucrats work in a style that can best be compared to juvenile fiction.

Bureaucrats, managers, or military officers (I've been all three) who think about turning to creative writing—either before or after retirement—can make good use of skills and habits they have already acquired or developed. First, we had to learn to write prolifically; there was no end to the documents we had to grind out. We've learned that the first draft is the hardest, so we push through it. We don't have time for writer's block; deadlines were tight and constant. We are used to showing our work to colleagues and to accepting criticism. Building consensus was part of the task.

However, we must make one major change in order to write credible fiction. We must adopt a more realistic tone. That is the hardest part.

—Von V. Pittman

Published in the July/Aug 2017 Issue of *Working Writer*

Breakfast at Earl's

Earl Perkins swung his three–foot length of half–inch pipe just as Matt scrambled into the back seat of my 1957 Chevrolet Bel Air. If he had not stumbled slightly, Perkins would have done considerable damage to both Matt and my beloved Chevy. As it was, he broke three bones in Matt's left hand and put a small dent in my fender. Matt screamed. Glenn pulled him in, then yelled, "Haul ass!" I did.

We could still hear Perkins yelling "snot–faced college pukes." I drove five blocks before stopping so that Matt could close the rear door.

Back in the early 1960s, the Ku Klux Klan was still a presence in Capital City. We had just pissed off one of its leaders. Perkins was rumored to be a Kleagle or a Cyclops for the northern quarter of the state. After this encounter, it would be best to avoid him.

During my junior year, Capital City—and thus Eastern State University—enjoyed the kind of perfect spring that comes along every decade or so. The superb weather, gorgeous plants and flowers, and ESU women in their sundresses created a setting that sapped many a college boy of all ambition. The temperature was warm, but never hot. Most nights a slight breeze floated soft scents of honeysuckle and wisteria. Back then, female ESU students were still required to live in dorms, and to be locked in them by 11:15 p.m. Males suffered no such restrictions. After female curfew, many males found gathering on the patios at Harry's or the Raging Goat to order "just one more" pitcher of Blue Ribbon preferable to returning to our squalid dorms or apartments. Usually around 1:00 a.m., somebody would say, "Anybody want to go for breakfast?"

Somebody always said, "Good idea."

Matt, a slender, hatchet–faced kid with red hair, chimed in "Damn straight," night after night. Then three, four, or five guys would head for one of the two greasy spoons or the one respectable café that stayed open all night.

One Tuesday in late April, I agreed to drive. Matt called "shotgun." James, who had come to ESU on a baseball scholarship, but hadn't made the grade, got in the back along with Glenn, a formerly devout Baptist boy who was enjoying a profound crisis of faith. "How about Earl's?" Matt said.

"You know Earl Perkins owns that place. And there are always a few of his Klan buddies there late at night," Glenn said.

"We've been there a lot," Matt said. "Nothing's ever happened. We've minded our business; they've minded theirs. We've never even spoken to each other."

I didn't want to look chicken. "Okay." I drove to the lower part of downtown, where Earl's All–Night Café sat on Hancock Street, between a tire recapper and the Western Auto. Inside, Perkins and two men in khaki work clothes were drinking coffee and smoking at the window table. We took the table farthest from them.

Glenda, an overweight night waitress who must have been in her mid–seventies, said, "What are you boys havin' tonight? Matt, I know you want two over easy and bacon." Glenda didn't have to ask us what kind of bread we wanted; all toast was white at Earl's. And grits came with all breakfast orders. James and I ordered scrambled eggs; Glenn made an exotic choice, French toast.

We overheard parts of the conversation at the other table. It sounded as if one of the men in khaki might be trying to sell Perkins a car. We couldn't be sure, and we didn't care. About the time Glenda arrived with our meals, Perkins and the two men stubbed out their cigarettes and walked into the kitchen. The conversation at our table turned to more important matters, such as the recent beer price increases in the local liquor stores.

As we finished our meals, Glenda came by to pour coffee refills. Three of us lit up Marlboros. Matt said, "I need to check out the men's room." When he returned, he said, "I think that window is just wide enough. All I have to do is step up on the toilet tank, pull up, and squeeze through. It opens onto the back lot."

"What?" I said. Then I lowered my voice. "You're not going to sneak out without paying, are you?" It took a moment to understand that he really meant it.

Glenn, too, was shocked. "Why?"

Matt practically snarled. "Because I got no money. Why else?"

Glenn was stunned. "Didn't you know that when you decided to come with us?"

Matt sneered. "Dumbass."

"I'll loan it to you until tomorrow," I said.

Matt scorned our naivety. "I already owe more than I can ever pay. To lots of people. Listen, all I want is for you to go up and pay Glenda, then walk out like everything is normal. Give me a couple of minutes, then pick me up around the corner on Harrison. I'll wait in the alley next to the dry cleaner."

We were whispering by then, even though there were no other customers and Glenda was in the kitchen.

"I don't like helping you steal," I said.

Matt scowled again. "I'll be in the alley. You can either pick me up or you can be chickenshit." He walked toward the men's room. The remaining three of us went to the counter to pay Glenda. I left her a bigger tip than usual.

Out on the street, James said, "You're gonna pick him up, aren't you?"

"I guess, dammit." I waited about a minute, eased away from the curb, drove slowly down Hancock, and turned right onto Harrison. As soon as we rounded the corner I could see Matt running up the street, with three men in hot pursuit.

Perkins yelled, "Damn college assholes. Stealing from workin' people." Fortunately for Matt, his pursuers were badly out of shape. He was pulling away from them." I caught up with Matt as Glenn threw open the rear right passenger door. Matt grabbed for the door opening with one hand and got the other on the top of the fender. Perkins swung the pipe.

Once safely away from Earl and his vigilantes, I said, "I heard that pipe hit my car. I'll bet you'll never pay for that, either." Matt just moaned.

"We'd better take him to Student Death," Glenn said, using the universal moniker for the University Infirmary.

When the nurse on duty saw Matt's badly swollen hand, she said, "What happened to you?"

James spoke up. "We were building a concrete block fence and I accidentally knocked over a block and it fell on his hand."

The nurse didn't buy it. "You were building a fence at three in the morning?" James shrugged. The nurse rolled her eyes. She told the clerk to summon the on–call x–ray technician and doctor.

The x–rays showed simple fractures of three left–hand metacarpals. The doctor told Matt, "Your hand is too swollen for a cast. We'll just splint and wrap it for tonight. I'm going to give you a few Percodans for pain. Take one now and one when you wake up. Then come back and we'll put a cast on.

When the nurse finished the splint, and Matt was beginning to feel the effect of the first Percodan, we walked to the car. Matt told us that he had gotten out the men's room window just fine, but Earl and his buddies had been in the lot, apparently looking over the car that was for sale. They had seen Matt come out of the men's room window. Earl picked up a piece of pipe and started chasing him.

Nobody said much of anything after that. I dropped James and Matt off at their dorm. I also checked the damage to my Chevy. There was a six–inch dent in the top of the fender, but the paint wasn't broken. I drove the half–mile to the dorm where James and I lived.

I decided to "get right" with the university. I started attending almost all my classes and confining my social life to the hours before midnight. I never ate at Earl's again. Glenn and I ran into each other in the dorm once in a while, but never had much to say. I never saw Matt or James again. However, the following fall semester I saw their names in the *Capital City Post*. The police had arrested them after finding a variety of stolen items in their apartment, including three payphones that had been torn off walls. My guess is that Matt and James didn't know that stealing public phones was a federal offense that could mean real hard time. I don't know if they went to prison; I never heard of either again.

A year later, I graduated from ESU and headed for the Navy. When I sold the Bel Air it still bore the dent Earl Perkins had put in it on a beautiful, wisteria–scented night.

No Greater Crime

"I hate murder investigations that involve professors!"

"Why's that, Sarge?"

"Too many plausible suspects, Tom. And this Professor Lamb seems to have had even more than his share. Who's first on your list to interview?"

"Lisa Manchester, a graduate student who filed a sexual harassment lawsuit against him."

"Nah. I know about her. She's had too much fun being the feminist heroine, expressing her outrage at every rally on campus. Besides, she was almost certain to collect a bundle in a settlement. Cut her loose. Who's next?"

"Assistant Professor Red Randall blamed Lamb for blocking his bid for tenure. Assistant professors—even those who oppose capital punishment—seem to think stopping someone from getting tenure justifies killing."

"Don't you ever read the university newspapers?" This tenure tussle has made Randall a hero–prof. He now sells himself as a champion of faculty rights, and the usual sorehead professors have bought into it. Besides, the provost is so chicken that he's telegraphing his intention to overrule the tenure committee. It ain't Randall, Tom."

"All these years on the force have made you pretty cynical, Sarge. So, how about Thaddeus Tharpe? Several profs and grad students have told me that he has always considered himself the world's greatest Benedict Arnold biographer, but now Lamb's new book on Arnold is getting great reviews and landing him a lot of speaking invitations and press coverage."

"That's not a bad start, Tom. But remember who we are talking about. If the murder weapon had been a cello, or maybe a volume of haiku, I'd think maybe it was Tharpe. But he wouldn't know which end of a softball bat to grip, much less how to take a horizontal swing, like he was at the plate. And whoever killed Lamb did precisely that. Anybody else got a beef against Lamb?"

"Not really, Sarge. I've heard references to one petty incident, something not even worth a good fight."

"Let's hear it, Tom. Right now, we've got nothing."

"Well, you know how all the history department's assistant profs have to park almost a mile from LaPlante Hall and walk from there? Then, they have to wait their turn—sometimes for years—for a spot in the lot next to LaPlante?"

"Yeah. So?"

"Associate Professor Alicia Watson's number had just come up, after waiting for three years. But Lamb went over to the Parking Office to check the records. He somehow bullied them into saying they had made a mistake; his number should have come up before Dr. Watson's. Parking Control took away her permit and gave it to Lamb. She was royally pissed off, I hear."

"He stole her parking space? Now you're talking, Tom!"

"But Sarge, you don't kill somebody over a parking space."

"You and I wouldn't. But these are professors, historians at that. They can imagine no greater crime. Stealing a parking space cannot go unpunished.

"But Sarge, . . ."

"Arrest her; cuff her; read her her rights."

The Interview

Having given up on a career as a historian, and thrown my hopes for a university career into the field usually called "continuing education," the time came to look for a job. Back then, continuing education departments were often known by such diminutives as "the academic third world" or "the Department of Everything Else," Names that said a great deal about the academic pecking order. But sometimes they were painfully accurate. For the greatest part, continuing education departments created and offered programs for working adults taking classes at off–campus sites or at night. They also offered "distance education" courses delivered by correspondence study and various television formats. In all these programs, the emphasis was on providing access to higher education to adults.

But there were exceptions. Many major university continuing education programs, particularly at land grant universities, offered high school diploma programs via correspondence study.

Originally designed for young students in rural areas—either to offer total diploma programs or to supplement the curricula of sparsely located country schools—some of them had huge enrollments. During the 1950s, for example, the University of Nebraska's correspondence high school called itself "the world's largest high school."

As noted, these correspondence high schools, operated by university continuing education departments, began as alternative formats for delivering high school diplomas. But other uses worked their way in. Students in conventional high schools who got behind by a course or two began taking correspondence courses to catch up. They could then transfer the course credits to their regular high schools. This means of catching up became known as "credit recovery." And it became extremely popular. Students in Florida could take correspondence courses from Louisiana State University, the University of Missouri, the University of Texas, or numerous other university–run correspondence high schools. And, importantly, the students were required to pay their tuition "cash on the barrel head" at the time of enrollment. Many, perhaps half or more, never finished their courses. Nonetheless, the enrolling school kept all of their money. This practice helped maintain the correspondence departments, most of which were required to operate on a financially self–sustaining basis.

Like my unemployed colleagues in history and other graduate liberal arts departments, I was desperate for a job. I would have considered any type of university continuing education program. The first interview opportunities I received were to direct university correspondence study departments, some with high school programs, some without. I gratefully accepted my first interview offer from Big Western Tech, in Lubbock, which operated one of the country's largest high school correspondence programs. I had heard of Western Tech, but knew nothing about it. I took a quick look at a map of the oil–rich Texas Panhandle, and found that it was about 100 miles each from Amarillo and Odessa. A flight to Dallas, then Lubbock, got me there on a hot Sunday afternoon, with the interview scheduled for Monday. As instructed, I took a cab from the airport to a generic motel near the BWT campus. It was not a short ride, but it was flat and barren. When we topped a railroad crossing, the driver said, "That's the highest spot in the county."

"Looks like a long way from Lubbock to anywhere," I said.

"It ain't but about a hundred miles to Odessa," he answered.

The next morning I was in my interview suit and ready to go when the interview chain began at seven. I soon became aware that my interview had been scheduled for the worst possible time. Every public high school in Texas held its graduation on the same day, Friday, four days hence. Thus, hundreds of Texas students who had enrolled in BWT correspondence study courses for "credit recovery," looking for the last one or two credits they needed for graduation were calling, or having the guidance counselors in their schools do so. I estimated that the high school office had roughly twenty–five operative phone lines, and they would all be busy through Friday. It was a matter of a time crunch. In other words, many—if not most—students had waited too late to get started. Most of them could have finished the twenty or so instructional units in their courses months earlier, then been in good shape for their finals. But that is not the way of credit recovery students. Apparently most still needed to turn in many instructional units—as many as a dozen—have them graded, then take their finals. I would learn that this was the way of high school correspondence programs all over the country.

This created all sorts of problems. First, the mails were not fast enough. There was no way to get a letter from Houston to Lubbock, for example in a day or two. Mommy and Daddy, who had already had to shell out extra money for tuition, now had to pay UPS or Fed–Ex to move the final exams from the BWT correspondence office to one of several dozen authorized examination centers across Texas. Then, the people at the centers had to be talked into providing numerous proctors to oversee the testing process, then to return the exams on the same day. This created huge demands on their staffs. And then, when the exam made its way back to the BWT correspondence office, Mommy and Daddy, the high school guidance counselors, and the students wanted to know if Darla June and Leroy had passed their finals, so they could get word to the high schools, so that the kids would be able to "walk," meaning to transit the stage and diplomas at the ceremony that night. All of this overwhelmed the office's staff and resources. "It will be like this until late Friday afternoon," one of the supervisors told me.

But before the hundreds of dramas could play out, someone had to grade and record the late–arriving instructional units and exams. The students, parents, and high school guidance counselors—many with furious parents breathing down their necks—expected the course instructors, all of whom were volunteers, and mostly part time, to drop whatever they were doing, grade Darla June and Leroy's finals, then report in to the correspondence office, which could then transmit their grades to high schools in McAllen, Lampasas, Alpine, Paris, Hamlin, Del Rio, Matchbox, and other Texas municipalities. I talked briefly to several instructors who had come into the office to drop off graded instructional units and exams. One said that an anxious father had driven 150 miles to Lubbock that morning, then tracked him down on the golf course, where he frantically harangued him to grade his daughter's geography exam.

Things didn't always turn out that well, of course. Another instructor told me about an occasion years before, when an angry father phoned him. When the instructor said that he had graded the exam, but his son had failed it, the father threatened that if the instructor didn't change the grade, he (the father) would dynamite his house! And indeed, credit replacement students often fell short when their work was graded. After all, these were kids who had gotten themselves into academic trouble in the first place through inattention, sloth, and indifference, and being just plain dumb. Many didn't find it difficult to fail final examinations. And beyond that, many had lied. For weeks, even a semester, they had told their parents that they were turning in their coursework. But many simply did not work on their courses. They had never turned in the lessons that were the prerequisite to taking the finals and earning credit. When the staff revealed that omission to furious parents, they could only imagine the dinner–table conversations around the Lone Star State, grateful that they were not participating in them.

The students who fell short of earning their necessary credit ranged from furious, to incredulous, to scared to death. All over Texas, relatives had come to town to attend Darla June and Leroy's graduation ceremonies. While this worked well for motels, parents did not see the humor in such situations. One indignant high school senior responded to the news that she would not be graduating that Friday night by telling us, "You can't do that to me; I've already had my hair done!"

The woman who was retiring as High School Correspondence Director was only able to give me ten minutes. She said she was too busy with calls. And she might have been. Either that, or she was just worn out and had become indifferent. The Associate Dean to whom I would have reported had I received an offer, "Mike," came by to pick me up to go to the University Club for lunch. He was accompanied by a nattily dressed man, probably in his mid–sixties, with a vague title, and introduced as "T.R." As new as I was to university administration, I had seen his type before. He had been, I deduced, a senior officer for many years, one who had done little for some time, who was replaced by new leadership. But instead of discharging him, the administration had shoved him sideways into a job with little responsibility and less authority. Entertaining out–of–towners was probably a frequent task. On the way to the club, I noted that the thermometer on a bank sign indicated 95F, yet I was still comfortable in my interview suit. "That's because the humidity is less than 10% today. That's what the weather is like on the South Plain, " T.R. said. I said that sounded pretty good to me.

"It is a pretty nice part of life here," he said, "but let me tell you about our dirt storms." He regaled me with horror stories of spring days of continuous dirt–filled air as he eased down a couple of bourbon and waters while his boss and I sipped vodka tonics. "Mike" seemed to know little about the detail–level operations of high school correspondence study. He was most interested in letting me know that he expected a larger financial return from that department. Overall, the Big Western Tech interview was probably the least intense and, I suspect, least serious interview I would ever have. At the conclusion of the meal/interview, T.R. dropped Mike off at his office, drove to the motel so I could pick up my suitcase, then took me to the airport, where we arrived two hours early.

"Good!" he said. Time for a few snorts before your plane." So we went to the VIP lounge, where he had three Wild Turkeys with water and I ordered one vodka tonic, then one straight tonic, and heard a couple of hours of Western Tech lore, but little about the job I had come out to interview for.

"Do the faculty and staff out here ever feel isolated?" I asked.

T.R. looked surprised. "Hell, it ain't but about 100 miles to Odessa."

~~~~~~

Western Tech did not make me an offer. The woman who got the job was a local, comfortable with the distance to Odessa, but without any background or qualifications in the field of correspondence study. I heard later from the guy who replaced her that she had had a nervous breakdown within a year.

Reduced Residency

This shouldn't be too hard. Spend a few minutes in the Special Collections room. Move into the Reference room. Pick up a book here, a reference volume there. Go to the Master of Fine Arts thesis section. Pick up one of the black volumes with gold lettering. The one you want will be right there. Nobody ever picks up these tomes. They were written by graduates of Wheelwright College's reduced residency MFA program. Like many small liberal arts colleges, Wheelwright has long offered master's degrees in education, mainly as an additional revenue stream. Then, like about thirty other colleges—mostly small— it added a reduced residency Master of Fine Arts program, also to raise revenue, and to add credibility to their claims to be graduate–degree granting institutions.

Reduced residency MFA students don't reside on campus. They live all over the country, and occasionally in other nations. They are assigned tutors—often part–time adjunct instructors—who work with them on a one–to–one basis, exchanging assignment drafts and critiques via mail, email, and scheduled telephone conversations. The students come to the campus, usually in the summers, for two short "residencies" of ten to fourteen days each. A thesis is required for graduation. But unlike other theses, they are not research–based. MFA candidates submit "creative" theses—novellas and novels, collections of short stories, works of creative nonfiction, and an occasional volume of poetry. They share one feature with conventional research–based theses—once shelved they are never read.

The fifty–three theses that have been submitted over the fifteen years the reduced residency MFA program has been offered at Wheelwright have all been shelved, but they have not been magnetized to trip the security system. Some past librarian had made security coding a part of the purchasing and receiving process. Since the MFA theses were never purchased, they never received a security code. And none had ever been stolen. As one exceptionally sensitive librarian once said, "Why would anybody steal that crap?"

You have work to do. Find R.B. Sadler, *The Homestead Fire*, in the theses section. Peruse it.

Try to look interested. Then look at your watch. Gather up your books, notebooks, and pens and place them in your old Land's End briefcase, along with the black–bound copy of *The Homestead Fire*. Walk out. Find your car in the main library parking lot, toss in your briefcase, then get in and drive away.

Don't go to Kinko's tonight. Go home and have a scotch highball. You deserve it. You can go to Kinko's tomorrow, or the next day. Nobody is going to notice the missing thesis. Go to Kinko's at the busiest time of day. Buy a card and copy away. Remember, *The Homestead Fire* is only 33,692 words. You can make short work of it.

But upon further consideration, why copy it at all? Why not just cut the pages away from the uniform black binding? Then put together enough blank pages, or pages you can find around campus that have been printed? They can be anything—curriculum plans, task force reports, or even drafts of strategic plans. For the sake of neatness, you might want to cover them with the old title page. Just tape the pages together and insert them into the black binding with the gold lettering. When you are finished, walk into the library and place the dummy thesis on a table. If the replacement pages should fall out someday, there would be no problem.

If someone should notice in five or ten years that the MFA thesis of one R. B. Sadler has been tampered with, so what? Nobody would even know who he—or she—was. A search of Wheelwright College's records would only reveal that Sadler was a male, that his home address was in Eufala, Oklahoma, and that he graduated in 2005. It would not be noted that he died in 2006. Professor Regina Simpson was his advisor. Many people at Wheelwright will remember that she was killed in a car wreck in 2013.

It is not as if R. B. Sadler had actually written the document, anyhow. By 2005, Rick was extremely sick, almost nonfunctioning. But his family hoped he could somehow graduate, perhaps with some kind of honorary degree. And you, too, wanted him to graduate. And so did Professor Regina Simpson, his adviser and mentor.

You pulled the *Homestead* draft of a novella out of your file cabinet. You had put it aside in frustration several years earlier, having failed to work it into publishable shape. You sent it, chapter by chapter, to Wheelwright's MFA program and Dr. Simpson. Simpson knew the work; the two of you had discussed it years earlier. For Rick's records, she briefly critiqued each chapter and returned it to you. Some of her criticisms seemed right on target. You used her suggestions when you liked them, ignored them when you didn't. Then she pushed the final draft past Rick's thesis committee.

Wheelwright conferred the MFA on Rick in December, 2005. He barely lived into 2006. Several years later, you heard from a mutual friend that Regina Sanders hit a utility pole head–on in her Audi. You figured that was the end of it. And it would have been if you hadn't had a sudden, urgent cash flow problem.

Now you have to steal your own work. But on the good side, you can now sell it over your own name. You are at the point at which your publisher will buy, print, and promote anything with your name on it.

Strange Bedfellows

"*That's* what voting means to you?"

Eric was faking his outrage, or at least half–faking it. "Don't act so shocked," I said. You're a mature adult, and an educated one at that, even if you did earn your degrees at this institution. You know politics isn't pretty. Functioning democracies are based on competing self–interests, modified and shaped by compromises made by ever–shifting coalitions."

Eric smiled, but rolled his eyes. "Yeah, but to vote a guy into office because he is a fool?"

"Not only a fool," I said, "but a liar, a screw–up, and an incompetent."

After a deep breath, Eric shook his head. "You know I don't have any more use for Thaddeus Tharpe than you do. I've been hoping like hell he would leave, get fired, or die, since the week he started here."

I had him thinking now. "Yeah. I know he's been a major pain to you. And think about our colleague Sarah. She openly wishes for his death."

"Well, you would, too, if he had accused you of sexually harassing him."

"He came pretty close. He claimed I refused to stop Sarah from harassing him," I said. That had been one of Thaddeus's more spectacular and outrageous stunts. It had started when I assigned Sarah and Thaddeus to a recruiting trip through Texas. I hadn't been aware this would be Thaddeus's first road trip with a woman as his partner. And that was of no importance in making the assignment. Like every large university, we send our Admissions staff on frequent recruiting trips in the fall, usually in sets of two or more. Teams often consisted of a man and a woman. Nobody had thought anything of it.

But the assignment had come as a shock to Thaddeus's wife Jean. We learned later that she had gone ballistic the night Thaddeus told her he had to go on the road with Sarah for five days. According to rumor, several figurines in the Tharpe house did not survive the night. Jean told him that he definitely was not going to make the Texas trip.

Thaddeus had come to me to say he could not travel with Sarah. When I asked why not, he said, "I'd be uncomfortable going on a trip with someone who wants me to go to a porno theater with her."

"What?" I dropped my feet off the desk and glared at him. "Sarah?"

"Yes."

"What the Hell did she say?"

"She said I had to go to a porno theater with her."

I had known Sarah eight years. This wasn't her. "Don't you think she was just joking? That sounds like banter to me."

"No. She said I had to meet her at a porno theater in Dallas."

"Thaddeus, what makes you think she could compel you to do anything like that?"

"She's my supervisor and she has five years seniority over me."

"And I have a lot more authority over you than that. Get your butt out of my office and get packed for the Great State of Texas! I'm not going to redo travel assignments because of your idiotic fantasies."

Then I went directly to Sarah's office and told her what Thaddeus had said. She turned red in the face, not from embarrassment, but from rage. I knew smoke would soon start billowing out of her ears. "What did you say to him?"

She said, "I told him I was going to spend a couple of hours in a fabulous women's shoe store near the convention center in Dallas. I said that it was just a couple of blocks away from a sports memorabilia store and a porno theater; he could kill time in either while I tried on shoes. It was supposed to be a joke, and a pretty obvious and lame one at that."

"So you never said he 'had to' accompany you to a porno show?"

"Goddammit! Of course not. I'm pissed off that you would even ask."

I slouched against her doorframe. "You have a right to be. I'm sorry, Sarah. And neither of you is going to like this, but I'm afraid I can't reschedule your trip. You two are just going to have to gut it out."

The next morning, Thaddeus filed a sexual harassment grievance against Sarah. He also named me for not putting an end to it. The case eventually worked itself out, with neither disciplinary implications nor satisfaction to either side. But it had eaten up a lot of time and caused a great deal of stress for Sarah and me. But of course, he got what he really wanted.

About six weeks later, for reasons unknown, Thaddeus actually apologized to Sarah for lying about her. He told her that Jean had made him do it, in order to get out of the trip to Texas with her. That's what having him in the office was like. He frequently slandered or lied to people, then expected them to understand, and even to sympathize. The porno theater was an extreme example, but not an isolated one.

Besides having a talent for stirring up trouble, Thaddeus was grossly incompetent. A couple of years after the incident with Sarah, I hired a team of admissions counselors from the University of Minnesota to inspect our staff's case files. While most of our admissions counselors had accumulated error rates of less than five percent in their correspondence with applicants, Thaddeus had approached an incredible sixty percent. I was sure that this would finally make it possible to fire him.

The disciplinary process leading to discharging an employee at our university had been devised not for the purpose of discharging incompetents, but rather to help employees improve their performance so that discharge would not be necessary. It assumed: (1) that the employee in question wanted to improve; and, (2) that the employee was capable of demonstrable improvement. Both assumptions rendered the process useless in Thaddeus's case. As I was just getting the paperwork started, the University Personnel Officer called me and warned, "If you spend about half a day on this matter, every day, it will take you about three months to complete it." That mad proceeding impossible.

And so it had come to this. I was calling my friends, colleagues, and family, trying to get them to vote for Thaddeus Tharpe for County Magistrate.

Thaddeus considered himself a "progressive activist," who could make a difference in county government. So when the incumbent magistrate announced his retirement, Thaddeus threw his hat into the ring. County Magistrate was a sort of glorified notary position that demanded little energy or intellect. But it paid about two thirds of what Thaddeus was costing us, and it required the officeholder to put in about six hours a day at the courthouse. He had told me at the beginning of the race that if he won, he would have to resign his position in University Admissions.

I was making the same pitch to Eric that I had already made to a couple of dozen people. "It is historically a low–turnout election. There is no incumbent. If the people in our office can round up a couple of hundred votes, we might be able to make the difference."

Eric shook his head. "Pretty sleazy."

I was not too proud to beg. "But this is going to be our only chance to get rid of him. Do you think any office on campus would hire this goof? If he wins, he goes away. If he loses, we're stuck with him forever."

"Point taken; I'll get Laura, too," Eric said, referring to his wife.

I was not the only one hustling votes. Sarah was passing out cookies with "Tharpe for Magistrate" buttons. Our office manager put

Tharpe campaign signs on her lawn and her son's.

I had no shame. I called my daughter, who was, I'm proud to say, a third–year student at Harvard Law. "Have you ordered an absentee ballot, Sweetie?"

"No, Daddy. Why would I bother for such a trivial election? Isn't it just for one magistrate and two county commission posts?"

I told her why.

"Daddy, are you trying to throw a fair election, to put in the poorest possible candidate instead of a perfectly adequate one?"

"That is precisely what I'm trying to do."

"But you have always told me about the genius of self–government," she teased.

"This *is* its genius," I insisted.

"I love it!" She said.

On election day, about a third of our office went directly from work to the polls, then to Paddy's Tap to wait for the returns. In such a small, lightly contested election, we expected the count to be completed early.

I was dripping sweat as I ordered my second, then my third Jameson's. Eric was making the rounds, talking it up, trying to keep spirits high. Sarah and her husband Tony were still, stone–faced, holding hands. At 8:52, the university FM station cut into its broadcast of the Pittsburgh Symphony to report the local returns.

The announcer gave the totals for the two commissioners' races first, even though everybody knew the incumbents would win in a walk. Then she said, "For the post of County Magistrate: Rhonda Perkins, 5,973; Thaddeus Tharpe, 6,007."

Some of us were slow in getting into the office the next morning. Paddy's had not closed its doors until 2:00 a.m. Eric and I were pasty faced. Sarah looked green. Someone had made a sign on our last remaining dot–matrix printer: DEMOCRACY TRIUMPHS! It was a great day.

We've only had one day that has even come close. A little over a year since the election, the town newspaper ran the headlines: "Wife Takes Shot at Local Pol," "Discovers Magistrate in Love Nest." That was a great day, too, even though Jean missed. But it was not as good a day as the one on which grassroots democracy truly made a difference.

Low Stakes

"We Know."

Penfield's knees buckled. He barely made it to the chair next to the faculty mail slots. "Are you okay, Sam?" Eleanor Gage, the history department secretary, left her desk and started toward him.

Penfield leaned back. "Yeah, thanks." He looked at the card again. The picture was a panoramic photo of Eaves Stadium at Eastern State University. On the reverse, his name and the address of Taliaferro College's history department had been typed on a label. Only the words "We Know," in twelve–point pica type, occupied the message space. He knew who knew.

Two years earlier, Dean "Skip" Rush had told Penfield that Taliaferro College could not renew his contract unless he started making progress toward completing his dissertation—and thus his doctorate—at ESU. Eighteen months later he had turned in a complete draft of his dissertation.

When he began to prepare for the following fall semester, he felt better than he had since arriving at Taliaferro in the summer of 1967. He also felt energized. The dissertation was no longer a gauzy mirage, barely visible over the horizon. Everything would be different. He and Becky could enjoy this fall. He bought tickets for two ESU games, Auburn on the road and Tennessee at home in Capital City for homecoming. They would make weekends out of the games, joining old friends from their undergraduate days.

For the first time, Penfield enjoyed preparing to teach his three fall semester courses. The work now affirmed his standing in the profession. Things could not get much better. Then they did. Dean Rush left a message for him to come over.

"Sam, we are proud of you. Once you got started on that dissertation, you moved right along. President Swift and I want to welcome you to the guild. Awarding tenure is just a formality. It will be taken care of shortly. Dr. Swift and I discussed your raise and came up with twelve percent, starting with your next check."

"Sir, I don't know what to say; that's terrific!"

Dean Rush beamed. "It's 'Skip' now, not 'Dean' or 'sir'. He walked around to the front of his desk and looked down on Penfield. "Sam, I rode you hard about finishing up the Ph.D. because I wanted you around for a long time. And so did

President Swift. If we hadn't seen something in you, we would have let you go.

At home, Becky said, "Sam, that's amazing! I'm so proud of you. Now the girls can get some cute clothes to go back to school; we can finally redo that torture chamber we call a kitchen. You've really turned things around for us. Once we get the girls down, I'm going to turn you around a few times." With the end of the doctoral ordeal Becky had become more spontaneous and frisky, like the long ago fall when they had met on a blind date for the Ole Miss game.

Because Becky kept her promise, Penfield ran late getting to his office. Eleanor finished sorting the mail just as he walked into the history department's office suite, feeling smug, whistling. Then he picked up the postcard with the picture of Eaves Stadium with its two–word message.

This message had to have come from a small group of malcontents who had been among his fellow history graduate students at ESU. None of them had yet gotten jobs. A few were stretching out their dissertations so that they could at least continue to pick up their miserable teaching assistant stipends for another semester, maybe another year.

Penfield didn't know them well. On trips to ESU, he had occasionally stopped by the graduate lounge while waiting to see Professor Stith, or to have a cup of coffee and a couple of Marlboros. There were always a couple of aging malcontents present. They seemed to do little but bitch about the faculty and the lousy job market.

"Sam, you're better off to avoid that bunch," Dr. Stith said. "They are bitter, burned out and, I'm afraid, finished. You were lucky to come along and get a job while they were still available to people with only master's degrees. Just a few years later, not only could master's graduates not get jobs, not even Ph.D.s could, at least those from third–tier institutions like this one. By 1970, the whole market was closing up tight, just about the time they were starting their doctoral programs. Several of these guys are as old as you. But they went to Vietnam about the time you went into your doctoral program.

Penfield said, "Are they likely to get anything, maybe at a community college?"

"Unlikely," Stith said. At least, not a permanent, tenure–track job. A couple of them are already working for community colleges, on a course–by–course basis, with no guarantees, no benefits, and no future.

"Why are they hanging on?" Penfield said. "Why don't they just give up and go into some other field while they still have time to start a decent career?"

"Those with any sense have," Dr. Stith said. "The hangers–on think their problem is the faculty's fault, that we don't try hard enough to place them. It's the school's fault because it's third–tier, instead of being Harvard. It's Nixon's fault; it's capitalism's fault. Hell, it's your fault. After all, you went out and took a job while the taking was good, when you could get a job first, and then finish your doctorate. Now you are nearly at the point of tenure and they never will be."

Stith picked up a pipe from his desk and pointed the stem at Penfield. "Sam, you are moving along pretty well on your dissertation. You have a job. You are damned lucky. But that's nothing to apologize for. Finish up the degree, get tenure up at Taliaferro. You can't help these guys; I can't help them. They are this generation's lost generation."

Knowing who had ruined the best school year of his life solved nothing. Indeed, it begged several questions. First, precisely which individuals were involved? How had they found out? Had they already had their fun, or did they intend to continue tormenting him? Would they expose him?

All his life, Penfield had lived with Calvinist dread. But now it had become an apocalyptic panic. After another week without a card or anything else from ESU, the panic receded to

41

manageable proportions. The following Tuesday, Penfield found a picture of the ESU chapel. Again, "We Know."

"Jesus H. Christ!" Penfield murmured. This was as bad as the first one, maybe worse. They were toying with him.

Spence had to be one of them. He had been a staff sergeant squad leader in the Americal Division, in the Central Highlands of Vietnam, directly responsible for the lives of nine men. He didn't say much about the war, mentioning it only in jokes about Army efficiency. However, the experience had apparently made adjustment to the low–stakes politics, professorial pomposity, and grad student obsequiousness of a university history department difficult. So he did not try. He exhibited open contempt for most of the faculty and many of his fellow students. Worse, as far as the faculty was concerned, he was a natural leader.

"I'm sure Mr. Spence had a rough time in Vietnam," Dr. Stith said. "But this isn't a war zone. It is a history department in a major university. He wanted the academic life; circumstances are forcing him out of it. I feel sorry for him, but his influence on many other students is disruptive. The sooner he is gone the better.

Costas or Lister, or both, had to be involved. Costas had been a naval officer for three years.

Lister was older, probably forty–five or more, a Congregational minister before coming to grad school. Like Spence, Costas and Lister were bitter and openly scornful of many history department professors and students.

When Penfield pulled the stack of mail out of Eleanor's hands Thursday morning, it included a card, addressed to him, with a picture of the Theta Chi sorority house at ESU. "We Know." Even if he had not grown up in a Presbyterian home, he would have known this problem would not end happily. But because he had been raised in that gloomy tradition, he knew for damned sure—with emphasis on the "damned"—he would have to pay. He had committed a grievous wrong. Actually, "wrong" didn't tell the story; it was a crime.

His tormentors gave him a week off, clearly intended to keep him on edge. He decided it could not go on. He had not had a relaxed minute since the first card arrived. His teaching stank. He was becoming short–tempered with the girls and found himself avoiding Becky's attention.

Penfield walked to the bookstore in the campus union and bought a postcard of Taliaferro's "Old Main." He sat down at a snack bar table, and addressed it to Roy Spence, at ESU's Department of History. He wrote "Let's Talk" in the message box. At the union's postal window, he bought a stamp, licked it, affixed it, and dropped the card into the slot.

Four days later, Eleanor was sorting the mail as Penfield arrived. She handed him a postcard featuring the ESU field house. The block printed message read:

2300, 17 September 1974
Waffle House, Panola Road

Penfield knew that Waffle House. It was one of half a dozen located on the Capital City beltway. They are going to demand money. Obviously I'll have to pay up. On the other hand they've got to understand that my resources are extremely limited.

On the 17th, he told Becky he was going to ESU to hear a lecture by Emory Thomas, one of the best–known active Civil War scholars. When he told her that he might be quite late, she was not pleased. His recent indifference to her advances had her on edge.

As he drove, Penfield tried not to reflect on the circumstances taking him into a scene with all of the congeniality of Hopper's "Nighthawks." When they left Capital City and ESU and moved to Plum Branch and Taliaferro, Penfield and Becky had initially settled into a lifestyle that could best be called placid. The girls liked their school, Becky found a half–time job in the local weekly newspaper office, and Penfield taught three history courses each semester. He also talked frequently about how he would complete his dissertation when he got settled in. At first he meant it. But the months moved by quickly; his courses and committee work took more time than he had believed possible.

The first semester at Taliaferro, he spent a few evenings trying to draft an outline of the dissertation topic he and Dr. Stith had agreed on, a biography of George Harrison, one of the many Confederate officers who later won a seat in the Alabama legislature and "redeemed" state government from "carpetbagger" control. Becky liked to make jokes about her husband writing a biography of one of the Beatles. Penfield never completed the outline. Other things always demanded attention.

When Dean Rush called Penfield in to talk about finishing up his dissertation, fear replaced idle hopefulness as a motivator. It was time to call his adviser. Dr. Stith, experienced in the ways of ABDs, agreed that it was time to find another topic. This led to several miserable weekends in the ESU library, hoping something would catch his eye. Nothing did.

One early spring weekend, Penfield grudgingly assented to Becky's suggestion that they take the girls to visit her parents in Opelika. In order to get out of his in–laws' house, Penfield drove to the Auburn University library, just a few miles away. Besides providing a way to get some peace and quiet, this reassured Becky that he was actually working on his dissertation, something she was beginning to doubt.

After an hour of idly scanning the library's Civil War–era holdings, Penfield reached the point he arrived at every weekend, wondering how long he had to stay to convince Becky he was working. He walked out for a cup of vile machine coffee and a couple of cigarettes. Walking back to the table he had staked out, he noticed the stacks where Auburn's dissertations and theses were filed. He found the history section and walked along slowly, glancing at the gold–embossed titles on the black spines. He picked one up occasionally and looked at the abstract. It was as good a way of killing time as any other.

The title of a master's thesis caught his attention: *The Etowah County "Plot": Slave Revolt or Tragic Rumor?* According to the abstract, rumors abounded that slaves on several plantations and farms had plotted a rebellion in Etowah County, Alabama, in 1842. As a result, anxiety among the white population escalated to the point that the sheriff and plantation owners and other white men in the part of the county around the towns of Boaz and Arab, rounded up around forty male slaves. They hanged four men and flogged another two dozen. But there was no investigation of the incident. No legal proceedings of any kind followed the executions.

The master's candidate who wrote the thesis, Cooper James, did not determine whether there had actually been a plot. According to the abstract, after a thorough examination and weighing of the available evidence, Cooper James could not definitively state whether there had actually been a slave plot in Etowah County. However, given the value of four able–bodied field hands, it seemed probable that the county's white population had devoutly believed that a murderous uprising was afoot. Hysteria— based on facts or not—had prevailed.

This was the most interesting thing Penfield had seen since starting his search for a topic. More importantly, it might be manageable. It ran only 150 pages. While provocative, its lack of a conclusion ensured obscurity. Given his needs, he did not want to create excitement or attention. Penfield took the thesis to his table and read it front to back.

After dinner that night, while Becky and her parents watched Dr. Zhivago on television, Penfield savored several shots of his father–in–law's Rebel Yell, a robust but rough bourbon still sold only in the eleven states that had seceded from the union. His thoughts were not in Tsarist Russia, but just a few miles away in Etowah County.

"Why don't you and the girls go to church with your parents in the morning?" For once, Penfield was not in a rush to leave Opelika.

"You sure, hon?" Becky said.

"I found some really good stuff today; I need to follow it up," he said. For the first time ever, they made love in her parents' house.

When the family pulled out for church the next morning, Penfield headed for a video game arcade. He bought two rolls of quarters, then headed for the Auburn library. He copied Cooper James's entire thesis, even his obligatory acknowledgment of the departmental secretary's help. Acutely aware of his lack of organization, Penfield used his remaining change to make a second copy of most of the first two chapters. Leaving the library he said, "Rubicon, baby!"

The next morning, Penfield called the Auburn history department. A receptionist named Cindy, with a cute southern accent, answered. "My name is Buddy Rogers," Penfield said. Cooper James and I are old friends, but we've lost touch. Is he still in your graduate program?"

"Coop–uh? He's gone," Cindy said. "We still miss him; he was funny. He finished up his master's and left here over three years ago. We heard he decided to go to law school over at Athens."

Penfield found an old University of Georgia

catalog and called the School of Law. The receptionist transferred him to the Alumni Office, where the receptionist sounded Canadian, Penfield decided. According to their records, she said, James had graduated, then joined the Navy's Judge Advocate General's Corps. His address was USS Mariana Straits, Fleet Post Office, San Francisco. "That's a ship," she said.

Perfect. There was almost no chance that James still cared who was doing what in southern history.

Plagiarizing proved harder work than he had expected. He started changing the name to Rumor or Revolt: The Boaz, Alabama 'Uprising.' He then began paraphrasing the Cooper thesis, sentence by sentence. Chances were slim that anybody beyond James's thesis committee had read it, but Penfield did not want to take even the slightest risk of triggering the memory of anyone on his committee. Paraphrasing soon became tedious.

When Dean Rush had pushed Penfield to get on with his dissertation, he told him to use the departmental secretaries to type his smooth drafts. So Penfield proceeded slowly through the first two chapters, paraphrasing the sentences, later marking errors or minor changes with a pen. He turned the draft over to Eleanor, who quickly typed flawless drafts he could turn in to Dr. Stith.

Penfield's habitual sloppiness and disorganization resulted in one early scare. While paraphrasing the second chapter, he realized that he had misplaced a page from the copied thesis. No sweat, he thought. I can pull that out of the partial second copy I made at Auburn. Then he couldn't find it. Had he left it at work, in the car? As panic began to set in, he found the missing page on his study floor, under some drawings his youngest daughter had brought home from school.

Dean Rush, President Swift, and Becky constantly asked, "How's the dissertation going?" Penfield became impatient and anxious. He began simply copying James's work, word for word. He did some marking up with a pen, so that Eleanor wouldn't notice a change in his pattern. His draft had to at least look new and rough.

"Here's chapter five, the last one, Eleanor." Penfield placed a folder on her desk with a flourish. "A month ahead of the deadline for spring graduation. All I've got to do now is write the acknowledgments. You'll see your name there."

"Well, thank you," she said. "But it will have to go through one more draft after your committee marks it up."

Penfield smirked. "The end is near, dear Eleanor. The end is near."

Dr. Stith moved Penfield's dissertation past an indifferent and barely conscious committee. That's when the good things started happening at Taliaferro and at home with Becky. And that was why—just a few months later—he was headed for a Waffle House late at night.

Penfield tried to relax his forearms; both had tensed up from gripping the wheel. Two thousand might satisfy these guys. I guess I might even raise another thousand with a personal note at the credit union. But it will be hell telling Becky she can't have her new kitchen. I'll try to lowball them. How did a few miserable teaching assistants figure it out?

He took the Panola Road exit and pulled up to the Waffle House. Three cars were parked at the back of the lot—the employees', no doubt. Three more sat near the building entrance. As he got out of his Nova, he saw two men in seed corn caps and overalls sitting at the counter, four empty stools between them. One was working on a hamburger and fries; the other stared over the top of his coffee cup. In the smoking section, in the last booth, Spence and Lister sat, with two cups of coffee, a pack of Pall Malls, a Zippo lighter, a half–filled ashtray, and a pair of half–moon reading glasses between them. Neither man stood as he approached. Nobody extended a hand.

As the waitress approached, Penfield said, "Just coffee."

Spence slid toward the wall to give Penfield room to sit. "You know we know or you wouldn't be here. But just to make things official, we brought you something." He handed Penfield the title page of Cooper James's thesis.

Penfield gripped the tabletop with both hands. "I don't think I could get more than a thousand or eleven or twelve hundred together, even if I tried to borrow some money. We overextended ourselves on our mortgage."

"Told you, Roy," Lister snorted. "I said this clown wouldn't be able to grasp any concept bigger than a few dollars."

Lister locked eyes with Penfield. "Just because you sold out doesn't mean the rest of us would." He picked up his reading glasses and gestured with them—an old pulpit habit. "Listen. I'll say it slowly. We don't want your damn money."

Things had just either improved or gotten much worse. Penfield couldn't tell which. "What do you want?"

"Your job," Spence said.

"What?" Penfield was as confused as he was shocked.

Spence took a Pall Mall from the pack, tapped one end on the Zippo a few times, then lit up. "You got your job dishonestly and dishonorably. It is time to open up that job for an honest historian."

Penfield could feel the onset of nausea. "If I were to leave, there's no guarantee that one of you, or anyone from ESU would get it."

"You think we don't know that?" Spence said. "It almost certainly wouldn't be one of us. But it would be someone who has written a dissertation."

Penfield wiped the sweat off his face. "My kids are in school. . . ."

"Oh," Lister said, "It's the old Shoeless Joe Jackson excuse: 'I done it for the wife and kids.' Listen. If you haven't submitted a letter of resignation before Tuesday, Dean Rush, President Swift, and the sanctimonious Dr. Stith, will all get copies of your last chapter, Cooper James's last chapter, and a letter. It won't take long for investigations to start. Taliaferro will fire you and ESU will strip your doctorate."

"And if I resign, you won't do that?" Penfield sounded almost hopeful.

"Right," Spence said. "You're finally catching on."

"But resigning is going to be hard to explain. How will I ever find a new job?"

Spence stubbed out his Pall Mall. "You'll do what your classmates are doing. You may try being a gypsy scholar, teaching a course at a time, wherever you can find it. You may turn to what our high–minded faculty calls "alternative careers," like working in the library or writing questions for the college testing companies. If you really hit bottom, you may try selling insurance. But you won't get any sympathy. Those are the same alternatives the rest of us are facing."

"It's not like I killed a man."

"No," Lister said. "It's worse."

Penfield sighed and leaned against the back of the booth. "How did you learn about this? I think you owe me that much."

Spence pocketed his Pall Malls. "You're a historian. You supposedly use evidence to reach conclusions. It will come to you."

Suddenly, no one had anything else to say. Spence picked up the ticket for Penfield's coffee. "On us."

Penfield's mind raced as he headed back onto the beltway. Then, as he accepted the reality that there was no way out, it gradually slowed down. He reached home in a near–catatonic state, totally exhausted. He undressed and slipped into bed without waking Becky.

The next morning he slept until ten o'clock, then took his time getting to the history department. Although he had missed his nine o'clock class, Eleanor seemed neither surprised nor alarmed. He poured coffee and went to his desk. Eleanor followed him. She placed two items on his desk. Pointing to the one on the right, a folder of papers, she said, "You left this when you gave me chapter one to type." It was the second copy of Cooper James's Auburn master's thesis, but without the title page.

The item on the left was a single sheet of Taliaferro letterhead, a perfectly typed letter of resignation, ready for his signature. "Eleanor!"

She placed her index finger under the lower–case initials that secretaries type two spaces below the signature line of letters: elg. "Look, Sam, it has my name on it."

A Talk with a Stranger

I fell in with a bunch of self–anointed pseudo–bohemians during my junior year at Drury. Back in 1963 all it took to be a rebel in Springfield was to stay up late at night and to occasionally talk about foreign films. Most nights at around one–thirty or two, somewhere between three and five of us walked to one of three nearby all–night restaurants. One February night only Alan and I decided to face the cold. We decided to go to Eddie's for French toast. One notch above a greasy spoon, Eddie's featured a strong, molasses–flavored syrup. Hank Williams dominated its jukebox. That night at about 2:30 a.m., almost nobody was there. Three night men from the *Springfield News–Leader* were taking their dinner break. A old man sat in a booth, sipping coffee and staring at a spot a thousand miles away. He shook the last cigarette out of a Pall Mall pack, lit up, then crumpled the empty pack.

He wore a pair of threadbare navy blue slacks,

a denim shirt with a bolo tie, and a wrinkled black jacket. His scuffed spectator wingtips were not a good match for his outfit or the gray fedora pushed onto the back of his head. A small straw and cardboard suitcase, with fake leather trim, sat beside him.

"What do you suppose his story is?" Alan said.

"Just a traveling man, down on his luck," I said. "He and his elegant luggage will be on the next Greyhound." Given that the bus station was less than two blocks down from Eddie's, that seemed about right.

"Wonder why he came through here?"

"Must be on his way to St. Louis."

Betty came and took our French toast orders. "Let's buy him a cup of coffee and see if he'll tell us his story," Alan said. If you bought a meal at Eddie's, Johnny, the night manager, would let the waitresses serve you as many coffee refills as you wanted. But if you came in and ordered only coffee, one cup was your limit. The old man was obviously resigned to this practice. He sipped infrequently and slowly. Alan went over to his booth and invited him to join us. Then he signaled Betty for more coffee. She looked toward Johnny, who gave a cursory nod. We were good customers. She poured a refill for the old man.

He said, "Appreciate it."

"Just passing through our fair city tonight?"

The man stared at his cup, probably wondering whether a refill was worth having to talk with two smartasses. I took a nearly full pack of Raleighs out of my jacket and offered him one. He took it, then tore the filter off. He pulled out a box of wooden matches and lit up. After a long drag, he said, "Thanks, partner." We waited him out.

Finally, he said, "Just did a show out in Carthage, out at the VFW post."

Alan took one of my Raleighs and lighted it with his Zippo. "You're in show business, then?"

The man placed his matchbox on the table. Using two fingers, he began to slowly push it around. He pushed it about three inches, up and down, left and right, in circles, all very slowly. Then it was gone! It was not as if the box disappeared. Rather, it suddenly ceased to *be*. We didn't know when it had gone away, and we sure as Hell didn't have any idea where.

"You're a magician!" I said.

"Good for you, Sherlock," he said. Then, suddenly, the matchbox appeared, spinning in the exact center of the formica tabletop, at least a foot from each of his hands.

"What's your stage name?" Alan said.

"The old man took another of my Raleighs. "Saving up ten thousand coupons so you can get an ice bucket or a set of barbecue grill tools?" The Brown and Williamson Tobacco Company used to attach a coupon to each pack of Raleighs, and four bonus coupons to each carton. Like S & H Green Stamps, customers could then trade the coupons for assorted items of merchandise.

"Since I spend money on cigarettes, I might as well get some of it back," I said.

The man rubbed his thumb across a lapel pin. Obviously cheap, it was black, with some of the enamel rubbed off. A plain capital "B" appeared in the center. "You didn't tell us your stage name," Alan said.

The magician pointed at the lapel pin, but said nothing. He held out his cup when Betty came by.

"Are you one of the Blackstones"? I said.

"Harry Senior's nearly eighty, but he's still performing out in Hollywood. Harry Junior's already doing big shows in Las Vegas. He's been on Ed Sullivan," said our entertainer.

"Are you a cousin or brother, or something?" I asked.

The man again touched the lapel pin with his thumb and winked. A worn pack of cards appeared out of nowhere. The man slid the deck in front of Alan and said, "Cut." At about the same time, he took another of my Raleighs, tore the filter off, and lit up. He shuffled, spread the deck and told me to pick a card—but not to let Alan or him see it—then slide it back into the deck. I did as he directed. Jack of Spades. He shuffled again, and again told Alan to cut. He again told me to slide a card out of the deck, then to leave it face down. I did.

"What card did you select on the first shuffle?"

"Jack of spades," I said.

"Turn your new card over."

I flipped the card. A Raleigh cigarette coupon was stuck over the card's face. After taking in our slack jaws for a few seconds, he pealed the coupon off to reveal the Jack of Spades.

"How the *Hell* did you do that?" Alan almost shouted.

The man stood up and pulled his fedora forward, brim over his eyes. "Bus leaves for St. Louis in ten minutes. Much obliged for the coffee." He picked up his suitcase, then opened the front door and turned right, headed toward the bus station.

"He never did say whether he was a Blackstone, or even a professional magician," Alan said. "We either met a poor relation from one of the most accomplished and professional families in magic, or the most skilled grifter I've ever run into." Alan liked to use words like "grifter."

"Whoever he was, he left with my pack of cigarettes," I said.

Two nights later, Alan and I, and two other aspiring hipsters, were at Eddie's eating French toast and listening to Hank Williams crooning "Lovesick Blues." Alan spoke up. "I called the Carthage VFW. They don't hire entertainers. They haven't booked an act in there since the Korean War. We were conned."

"So what?" I said. "It was the cheapest con we'll ever run into. That old man was the best sleight–of–hand artist I've ever seen. And the price was right, a cup of coffee and a pack of cigarettes. Less than a buck altogether. That's not too bad a loss to a down–on–his–luck grifter. And how the Hell did he stick that Raleigh coupon onto the Jack of Spades? I'm smoking Marlboros from now on."

Tommy Hawk's Boys

Both deputies were big men. The larger one, who looked like a central casting version of a rural lawman, stepped between the four of us and the front door of Frost's Truck Stop. "Would you boys mind steppin' away from the door a little bit? We'd appreciate it if you could wait here with us a few minutes. Four boys robbed the University Hotel and the campus police are bringing the desk clerk out to identify you." He did not add, "or rule you out." This couldn't be good.

As of the beautiful spring of 1965, the 1960s had not arrived in Capital City. They wouldn't be there for another four or five years. True, Eastern State University had finally begun to admit African–American students eight years earlier, but so far only a handful. Compared to the town, however, the university was considered a hotbed of liberal thought and activity, usually called "outside agitation." And tonight we were outside even the relative safety of the campus and the city. We were in territory called, "the county."

Out here, Sheriff Tommy Hawk's deputies reigned, easily identifiable by their khaki shirts, brown slacks, and straw "Smokey the Bear" hats. They liked to hassle college students, especially in front of redneck audiences.

In my second year at ESU, I spent the spring semester going through what counseling psychologists and student affairs bureaucrats called a "developmental task" typical of post adolescent males. My mother would have called it just a phase if she had known about it. It consisted mainly of falling in with a dubious crowd, then reversing the clock. Later, someone from the Dean of Students office would tell me that "task" had to do with establishing my autonomy and becoming an adult.

My developing autonomy had put me on a new schedule. After rising with great difficulty and numerous curses, I dragged myself to a 10:00 a.m. class. Rank vending machine coffee and five or six Marlboros or Old Golds helped me get through it. Back then, about a third of the students in a given class lit up, and many professors smoked as they lectured.

After that class, I returned to my room in Payne Hall, drank a Fresca and ate a Snickers bar, then went to sleep until just before my afternoon classes. When they ended at four o'clock, my day really started. Ma Dean's boarding house sold a twenty meal ticket for twenty–five bucks. One serving of meat, with unlimited vegetables, bread, and iced tea made it a good deal. The time between leaving Ma Dean's around 5:30 p.m. and getting back to the dorm—or "residence hall" in today's jargon—at about 8:00 p.m. just disappeared. Looking back, I can't account for that time.

Once back in Payne Hall, my main activity was a kind of active and social procrastination. If other residents didn't stop at my door to talk, I went in search of other open doors. It was usually easy to find enough other wastrels to start a game of poker or hearts. Studying might start at around midnight, if I wasn't in the middle of a novel.

At about 2:00 a.m., four or five regulars from the band of borderline miscreants and marginal students I had fallen in with would drive to one of the three local restaurants that stayed open all night. The Dogwood, on Broad Street, served great French toast and Hank Williams ruled the jukebox. Patsy Cline held that position at Earl's, over on Calhoun Street. Or if time wasn't a problem—and it usually wasn't—we could take Highway 40 out into the county and eat at Frost's Truck Stop, where all the present and past stars of country music could be heard.

I usually had scrambled eggs and sausage patties at Frost's. Grits came alongside. "Toast or biscuits?" the waitresses asked. "Toast" meant white bread; there was no use asking for wheat.

By 4:00 a.m. we were back in our dorms, where we slept until the hour we had to choose between crawling out of bed for the first class of the day or skipping it again. If I decided on the former, I bought machine coffee and lit the first of the day's forty or fifty cigarettes.

Following one particularly beautiful day we decided to head out the highway for Frost's. I drove that night, in the '57 Chevy 210 four door I loved more than I had once loved Cindy, my high school girlfriend.

Frost's was doing a great business for the middle of the night. It was about half full of truckers and textile mill workers who had just ended their shifts, along with the usual ne'er do wells. Our Bermuda shorts and polo shirts marked us as the only ESU students present.

For some reason, we felt particularly silly that night. Instead of talking about tough courses, unreasonable professors, and the price of beer in the various small towns surrounding Capital City, we got onto the subject of how guys could shock and embarrass the girls they dated. During this high–minded discussion, an argument broke out as to whether it was easier to humiliate a long–time girlfriend or a blind date. In short, we were living down to the stereotype of college boys held by many of our fellow diners.

Paul, an econ major and the oldest of us, described how one guy had embarrassed his girlfriend with a reference to her heavily padded bra while they were out at dinner with several other couples. From this relatively elevated plane, the discussion went downhill.

Matt, a razor–thin redhead from Arkansas, said, "We should write a book, *One Thousand and One Ways to Gross Out Your Date.*" Stories gushed out, punctuated by whoops and belly laughs. Some stories were old myths; a few were new. Some may have even been true. We got even more raucous until we noticed the two large Carlisle County Sheriff's deputies. We quickly piped down. Possibly some Frost's employee had had enough of our tomfoolery and called them. We drained our coffee cups, stubbed out our cigarettes, and walked to the cash register to pay up.

When Sheriff Tommy Hawk's boys told us why they wanted us to stick around, I was relieved. They hadn't come out here for a routine recreational roust of college boys. And of course we had nothing to do with a robbery. So we moved away from the door, as requested.

Paul, who had a year on the rest of us, whispered, "You know they can't make us stay here unless they arrest us. All we have to do is ask, 'Are we under arrest?' If they say we aren't, we can just walk out."

"We all know that," I said. "But I don't want to take a chance on Tommy Hawk's boys' knowledge of the Constitution."

"Tommy Hawk's boys have probably never even heard of the Constitution," Matt said. "And if they have, I'll bet they disapprove of it."

"Yeah," I said. "Let's just sit tight."

Today the Eastern State University Police Force is a highly professional outfit. Such was not the case in 1965. Then they were mainly in the business of being night watchmen and controlling traffic. Instead of driving standard police cars, like Crown Victoria's, they scooted around in Ford Econoline pickups, funny little flat–nosed vehicles with the engine housed in the cab, between the driver's and passenger's seats. They used them mainly to move traffic barricades around. The campus cops wore white shirts, black clip–on ties, and military styled caps. Only their Smith and Wesson .38 caliber revolvers saved them from looking like 1950s milkmen.

When the campus police Econoline pulled into Frost's parking lot, cops sat in the driver's and passenger's seats. A young man in civilian clothes, obviously the desk clerk, was perched on the engine. As the three men got out of the tiny pickup, all four of us looked out through the plate glass window. The clerk immediately yelled so loud we could hear him inside. "God dammit!

67

I told you they was colored." But he didn't say "colored."

We heard no apologies. The deputies went out to talk with the witness and the campus cops. The four of us said nothing to any of the lawmen. Without asking permission, we got into my Chevy, rolled the windows down, and pulled away. I stayed five miles under the speed limit until we were back in the Capital City limits. Then Paul yelled out the window, "God dammit! I told you they was colored!" And he said "colored." We had left two of Tommy Hawk's finest with red faces. As Matt said, "only the evidence saved us."

The Trail of the Ferret

October 16, 1979

Walter Sanders, Ph.D.
Executive Vice President
Eastern State University
Capital City

Dear Dr. Sanders,

I need to graduate from your university by this time next year. Since coming to Big Mound State Penitentiary, I have earned thirty–five semester hours of college credit and the Associate of Arts degree through Big Mound Community College's branch campus here. Also, I have earned the A.B. and M.A. in Sociology from Northwest University in Spokane (not traditionally accredited). I began studying sociology because I like to study groups of people. I have also received the Juris Doctor from the Crater School of Law, in Chicago, and the Doctor of Divinity from the C. H. Holly Theological Seminary in Nashville.

The state Board of Pardons and Paroles met in February, 1979, to decide my petition for parole. The Chairman (head) of the Parole Board, George Johnson, said I would be a danger to society with my education and a fifteen–year–old conviction of embezzlement. He said I should obtain a more traditional education if I want to work in regular society. It would meet the standards and requirements of the Parole Board better than my diplomas from Northwest University, Crater Law School, and Holly Seminary.

So I went to court with them (remember my law degree). The court upheld their end, in State Supreme Court 57194. The Parole Board is now deciding in my case what should be considered rehabilitation of a prisoner.

Now if I return to school as suggested by the Parole Board, that would be against my own ethical system. I believe my degrees are as good as your school's degrees. But it looks like the only way I'll ever get the hell out of here is to play the Parole Board's game. Eastern State University's Bachelor of General Studies, offered here at BMSP, is the only traditional program accessible to me. I need to graduate in May or June of 1980. That would mean that I have to take all four of your courses offered here each semester, as well as some of your correspondence courses. But that would not be a problem. I'm capable of doing a lot of work.

Another degree will certainly not hurt me, but I will need ESU's help. The prison's education allowance, including the federal BASIC Grant, will only cover about half the tuition for the courses here at the BMCC site inside the penitentiary. And it will not cover any of the correspondence courses. So ESU will have to waive or pay the tuition for them as well.

You need to be aware that the Parole Board's specification that I be given the opportunity to get a traditional degree, through a traditional institution, has the weight of a court order. So ESU <u>must</u> waive or cover whatever tuition the federal government won't take care of.

Certainly more education—either traditional or nontraditional—will never hurt a person in rehabilitating himself. I am 38 years old. For me, the degrees I have now hold the key to my future, but the Parole Board says I must attend <u>your</u> school! I am enclosing copies of all my transcripts. I anxiously await your answer.

Cordially,
Robert Raymond, Ph.D., JD, DD

October 20, 1979
Mr. Robert Raymond
P.O. Box 520
Midville

Dear Mr. Raymond:

I have received the letter related to your wish to earn Eastern State University's Bachelor of General Studies program, offered at the Big Mound Community College branch campus at BMSP. I am referring your letter to Dr. Lou Greene, Director of our Department of Off–Campus Programs. He will provide you information about our program at BMSP and see that both conventional and correspondence courses are made available to you.

If you would like to make application for admission to Eastern State University, you should contact Ms. Cynthia Holder, our Director of Admissions. She can provide you with the information and forms necessary to complete your application.

We encourage you to continue your efforts to secure a more traditional education and we hope you will succeed.

Sincerely Yours,
W. Sanders

cc: Lou Greene, Cynthia Holder

MEMORANDUM
DATE: October 20, 1979
FROM: Walter Sanders, Executive Vice President
TO: Lou Greene, Director of Off-Campus Programs
SUBJ: Please handle

Please respond to the attached letter from Robert Raymond, an inmate at Big Mountain State Penitentiary. Mr. Raymond wishes to attend—and hopefully to graduate from—the ESU off-campus program your office coordinates there.

I have attached a copy of my response to Mr. Raymond, as well as his inquiry and a number of enclosures, including copies of transcripts.

MEMORANDUM
DATE: October 22, 1979
FROM: Lou Greene, Director, Department of Off-Campus Programs
TO: Cynthia Holder, Director of Admissions
SUBJ: Robert Raymond's Application

For some reason, Vice President Sanders sent the copies of Robert Raymond's transcripts to me. They obviously should have gone to your office. I did take a look at them, however. The associate of arts from Big Mound CC is legit. Raymond took all of his semester hours through BMCC's penitentiary campus.

Raymond's other degrees, the two in sociology, the law degree, and the Doctor of Divinity are more interesting, and of course, bogus. Northwest University, Crater School of Law, and Holly Theological Seminary are all unaccredited correspondence course mills. While they list addresses in Spokane, Chicago, and Nashville, all three schools operate out of the same "campus" in Spokane, Post Office Box 59423.

"Dr." Raymond must be a remarkable student. He completed all of his "nontraditional" degrees in just sixteen months! He impressed the faculty and administration at Northwest University so much that they made him their "Assistant Director of Admissions for the Midwestern Region." Isn't it amazing that he can hold down such a complex job while incarcerated?

It looks as if you will have to admit this felon–American to our Bachelor of General Studies program at BMSP. We let in worse students every day. And students at BMSP are nothing if not litigious. We have to deal with frivolous cases from there all the time. Remember, he's a "lawyer."

If you admit Dr. Reynolds, expect him to ask you for money. If you say "no," be ready for him to threaten to sue you. That is the world in which our student–felons live.

From a handwritten note on a half-sheet of green scratch paper, undated, attached to an October 25, 1979, memo from Cynthia Holder to Lou Green:

Lou, be more careful when you put things in writing. I doubt Dr. Sanders would be amused by "felon–American." And as you noted, litigation might someday be in the picture with this guy. If so, we would have to pull all the paperwork on him from our files and turn it over to him.

Tear up this note! My attached memo is the official word.

He's your problem now. C.

MEMORANDUM

DATE: October 25, 1979
FROM: Cynthia Holder, Director of Admissions
TO: Lou Green, Director, Off-Campus Programs
SUBJ: Admission of Robert Raymond

I have forwarded a copy of my letter of acceptance to Robert Raymond, effective Spring Semester. Given his BMCC credit hours, and our augmentation agreement, he is qualified to pursue an undergraduate degree. Because Mr. Raymond intends to take some of his work via ESU correspondence courses, he may enroll as soon as he wishes.

Like all students who register at off–campus sites, I notified Mr. Raymond that he should contact your office with respect to all administrative matters.

October 25, 1979
Mr. Robert R. Raymond
P.O. Box 520
Midville

Dear Mr. Raymond:

Congratulations! You have been admitted to Eastern State University, effective Spring semester, 1980. We have examined your transcripts and have accepted sixty–two hours of transfer credit from Big Mound Community College. Therefore, you will enter ESU at the junior level.

Because you plan to register and take courses at an off–campus site, ESU's Department of Off–Campus Programs will be in charge of all administrative details related to your degree program. Please contact them with any questions or concerns.

Good luck, and GO Jackrabbits!

Sincerely,
Cynthia Holder
Director of Admissions

October 27, 1979

Mr. Louis Greene
Director of Off-Campus Programs
Eastern State University
Capital City

Dear Mr. Greene:

You should be aware that I have been officially admitted to ESU's Bachelor of General Studies Program. As I have communicated with Vice President Walters:

1. I must take several ESU correspondence courses in addition to all the courses that ESU faculty will offer here at BMSP, and,

2. I do not have the funds to pay for either the correspondence courses or the fifty percent of tuition that the federal BASIC Grant program does not cover. However, in my case this should no longer be an issue. Not only has the State Board of Pardons and Paroles ruled that I must be given access to courses and a traditional degree program, ESU Vice President Walter Sanders stated that "Mr. Green will see that both conventional and correspondence courses are made available to you."

I want to start my correspondence courses <u>now</u>. My course selection forms are enclosed. Thus it is imperative that you enroll me immediately!

I will be keeping Parole Board Chairman George Johnson and ESU Vice President Sanders informed of my progress, via copies of my correspondence with you and others at ESU.

You should also know that if necessary, I will contact the Presiding Judge of the Fifth Circuit with respect to the Parole Board's order, pursuant to State Supreme Court 57194.

Regards,
Robert Raymond

p.s. You know that I hold a doctoral degree. Therefore, please address me henceforth as "Doctor Raymond."

October 31, 1979
Dr. Robert M. Raymond
P.O. Box 520
Midville

Dear Dr. Raymond:

Congratulations on your admission to ESU. But don't get your hopes up for the Jackrabbits. I think they're going to have a tough season.

You may be surprised to learn that I, too, have been awarded a doctorate. While the University of South Carolina may have conferred it mainly as a means of inducing me to leave Columbia, it is nonetheless a Ph.D. Thus, I will be happy to address you as "Dr. Raymond," but only if you will return the favor.

I regret that my office will be unable to enroll you in any correspondence courses until you send a check to cover tuition and textbooks. Unlike other ESU courses, correspondence courses require 100% payment up front. When Dr. Sanders told you that ESU courses would be made available to you, he meant on the same basis as to all students—payment in advance—cash, check, or credit card.

To this point, my office has received no notice, court order, or other papers pursuant to your case "State Supreme Court 57194." Is it possible that you may have misunderstood the decisions and/or instructions of the Board of Pardons and Paroles?

Thank you for choosing an Eastern State University off–campus program.

Cordially,
Louis Greene, Ph.D.

Cc: Gabriel Erickson, Coordinator of Education, BMSP

November 3, 1979
Gabriel Erickson, Director of Education
Big Mound State Penitentiary
Midville

Dear Gabe:

Thanks for lining up the same classroom for all four of our ESU courses next semester. For whatever reason, all of our instructors say they feel safer in Room 4 than in any of the other classrooms. I know you have to schedule everything from elementary school classes up through college. So thanks for helping us out.

I need to check with you about a new Jackrabbit in your fold. This week we admitted "Dr." Robert Raymond to our Bachelor of General Studies program. Besides claiming a M.S. and a D.D., he says he also has a law degree (all from correspondence diploma mills). While interesting," this is beside the point.

Raymond says there is a "court order" (or something) in force that entitles him to an entirely free ESU education. He wants not only free admission to our courses offered in your facility, but also our correspondence courses, which we run on a cash on the barrelhead basis. I told him I haven't seen a court order or any other legal documents. Now he is making threats and says he is writing judges.

It might be best if we could discuss his case on the phone. Could you please call at your convenience?

Thanks,
Lou Greene, Director of Off-Campus Programs
Eastern State University

November 6, 1979
Ferris R. Fain, LLD
Presiding Judge, Fifth Circuit
Capital City

Dear Judge Fain,

I am writing to you as the Presiding Judge in the circuit that Eastern State University is located in. I am enclosing copies of several documents that provide background for my case.

Last summer the Board of Pardons and Paroles considered my suit requesting immediate parole. The Board deferred my petition, but ruled that I needed to attend a "traditional degree program" in order to prepare for my chosen profession in social work. I applied for the only accessible program of that kind. It is offered by Eastern State University here at BMSP. Therefore it is incumbent upon ESU to provide me full access. And indeed, ESU has admitted me to its bachelor's program. (See enclosed copy of letter of acceptance.)

That brings me to the crux of my problem. No one at ESU has made the required financial arrangements to cover my tuition and book costs. As best I can tell, my case has been delegated to a minor functionary named Louis Greene. He has done nothing to arrange for the payment or waiver of my tuition. I've notified him of the

Parole Board's ruling in my case, State Supreme Court 57194, as well as the steps ESU must take in order to comply with it. Mr. Greene has done nothing! He continues to say that it is necessary for me to come up with the full tuition in order to enroll.

I would appreciate it, Judge Fain, if you would contact the senior ESU official that I referred my case to in the first place, Dr. Walter Sanders, the Executive Vice President. Unlike anyone else at ESU, he encouraged me to pursue a traditional degree at his school. He also assured me that the necessary classes would be made available to me. I'm sure that he does not realize that neither Louis Greene nor the Director of Admissions, Cynthia Holder, has done anything to comply with the Parole Board's mandate to provide me with financial access to ESU's program at BMSP.

Thank you for your attention and interest. I am confident that as a fellow member of the legal profession, you will understand my frustration.

Cordially,
Robert Raymond, JD

From the Telephone Log of Lou Greene:

CALL FROM: Gabe Erickson
DATE: 11-9-79, 0935

GE calls Raymond "the Ferret." Looks more like a ferret than any human he has ever seen.

—Said "a con man is a con man." Reynolds is in BMSP for swindling. Other inmates hate him; he tries to run cons on them. Only reason they don't kick his ass is because he is a "lawyer," who may be able to help them.

—So called "court order" is just the informal advice of Geo. Johnson, Chair of Parole Board. He told Reynolds to "quit screwing around and get a real education." There is no legal significance to this "advice." Johnson was just blowing him off.

—Said I should get used to Ferret's (Raymond's) games. Will try to con our instructors, administrators, anyone else. Skilled in misconstruing conversations and correspondence. Says <u>be very careful</u> with anything we put in writing.

—Said he would send me a picture of Reynolds. Suggested I find a photo of a ferret and see if the two don't match. Assures me they will.

November 13, 1979
George Johnson, Chairman
State Board of Pardons and Paroles
Capital City

Dear Mr. Johnson:

I hope you can help me with what I believe is a minor matter. An inmate at BMSP, Mr. Robert Raymond, maintains that he is being denied access to an Eastern State University degree program that you and the Board of Pardons and Paroles mandated for him, pursuant to State Supreme Court case 57194. In a letter to me, Raymond maintains that as a result of the findings, one state agency—ESU—should pay for—or obtain a waiver from—expenses levied by another state agency, Pardons and Paroles.

I know of no legal means by which one state agency can compel another state agency to expend its appropriated funds for a specific purpose. Mr. Raymond assures me that you issued such an order. Can you—informally—shed any light upon this matter? I would hate to have a case that looks so dubious lead to further waste of this state's time and money.

Thank you for your attention to this matter.

Sincerely,
Ferris R. Fain
Chief, Fifth Judicial Circuit
Capital City

11-9-79
Mr. Louis Greene
Department of Off-Campus Programs
Eastern State University
Capital City

Dear Mr. Greene:

You need to know that you are in jeopardy of encountering serious legal liability. I have notified you of the outcome and judgment of my parole hearing, and the order of Executive Director George Johnson, pursuant to State Supreme Court Case 57194. To this point, you have taken no steps toward compliance with the Board's mandate that I be given full access to ESU's Bachelor of Liberal Studies program. I have notified Executive Director Johnson of the Parole Board of your failure to comply with its order. I have also initiated a petition for relief from Chief Justice Ferris Fain of the Fifth Circuit.

If I do not hear from you this week that you have cleared the way to my enrollment, I will contact Vice President Walter Sanders at your institution. He is the official who first pledged to make ESU's degree program available to me.

I am aware that you are a low–grade functionary with just enough authority to snarl the red tape. But you can do so only as long as nobody but the victims of your indifference and lack of accomplishment is paying attention. I advise you to get busy. Your boss, Vice President Sanders, is not going to like getting inquiries from the state judiciary and other persons of high authority. Think about this, then do your job.

Robert Raymond, JD, DD

November 9, 1979

Ferris R. Fain
Chief, Fifth Judicial Circuit
Capital City

Dear Judge Fain:

I am writing in response to your letter of November 9.

Robert Raymond is currently an inmate in the maximum security unit of Big Mound State Penitentiary. Mr. Raymond likes to reference State Supreme Court case 57194. This makes no sense. The Court actually denied his petition for the reversal of one of his convictions, and for immediate release. In short, Mr. Raymond lost that suit, without qualification. This was one factor in the Board of Pardons and Parole's denial of his petition for parole. While there is no point in going into detail here, there were additional factors in our unanimous decision.

Upon hearing the Board's decision, Mr. Raymond yelled out a question something like, "What do I have to do to get out of this place?" He recited his list of his diploma mill degrees. I suggested that it might help his cause to pursue a legitimate degree through a more traditional institution. However, I certainly did not promise parole if he should achieve that goal. And frankly, given Mr. Raymond's history of fraud, I am dubious about his ability to earn a degree from a legitimate school. His current attempt to "game" Eastern State suggests that he would not. The state's penal system is required to confine Mr. Reynolds and provide for his basic needs until he is either granted parole or until he serves his entire sentence. No other state agency has any responsibility to serve him.

Eastern State University cannot be commanded to provide scholarships or any other form of financial assistance to Robert M. Reynolds. I will notify the appropriate persons at BMSP and ESU by copy of this letter.

Cordially,
George Johnson, Chairman,
State Board of Pardons and Paroles
Capital City

cc: Gabriel Erickson, Coordinator of
        Educational Programs, BMSP
        Louis Greene, Director of Off-Campus
        Programs, ESU

December 10, 1979
Dr. Lou Greene, Director
Department of Off-Campus Programs
Eastern State University
Capital City

Dear Lou,

This holiday season brings early good tidings for you, but sad tidings for our Ferret. Almost a year ago, another of BMSP's residents, Mr. "Bloody Butch" Patterson, retained the services of our favorite attorney, Robert Reynolds, Esq. Bloody Butch, one of our most colorful (and deadly) residents, read an article on writs of *habeas corpus.* I believe he found it in either *Reader's Digest* or *Popular Mechanics.* According to the article, some jailhouse lawyer, somewhere, submitted a writ of *habeas corpus* that actually led to the eventual release of a convicted multiple murderer.

Bloody Butch, the head of BMSP's biker gang (yes, we have a biker gang; don't ask), thought this sounded pretty good. Several months ago he decided that the Ferret should write and submit a petition for a writ of *habeas corpus* that would spring *him.* This scheme might have been a tad unrealistic since Butch was convicted on three counts of first–degree murder. Indeed he would have been on death row if our state still practiced capital punishment. As I heard it, attorney Raymond initially declined to represent Mr. Patterson, presumably because his case for release was preposterous, and because the Crater School of Law had not prepared him for work of such gravity. Patterson responded by breaking the Ferret's nose and blackening both eyes. Raymond had a sudden change of heart and agreed to take the case.

Raymond put in hours and hours, then more hours, in our law library (state penitentiaries, by law, are required to maintain them), writing draft after draft of the petition for a writ of *habeas corpus.* Finally, he showed a badly typed document to Butch, who went to a former warehouse clerk on his cellblock who agreed to retype it, as an alternative to having his fingers broken. Butch then submitted the document to the Third Circuit.

Late last week the Court returned Butch's petition, denying it without comment, except to note a total lack of merit. Convinced that his case did indeed have merit, Bloody Butch was peeved. He decided the court had rejected his petition due to inferior representation; his attorney had not adequately conveyed the merits of his case. After knocking half the teeth out of the Ferret's head, Butch threw him down two tiers of the steel stairway in Cell Block Three, breaking both arms and causing serious internal injuries.

In a day or two, the Ferret will be transferred to the penitentiary system's hospital unit in Goodrich, up in the northwest corner of the state. Thus, I must regretfully notify you that he will be unable to attend ESU classes here in our Big Mound unit.

I don't usually write such long letters, but once in a while it is so rewarding that I can't stop myself. On the way home today, stop at the best bar along the way and lift a glass of Haig and Haig to the legal profession (I've already done so). May it always prosper!
Gabe

Handwritten note on a Christmas card from Lou Greene:

Dear Gabe:

Thank you so much for the good tidings in your holiday letter. It is a shame that Mr. Raymond's pursuit of higher education has been interrupted due to reasons of health. To paraphrase Gilbert and Sullivan, a ferret's lot is not a happy one! Thanks for your help over the past months.

My extended meeting with the Messrs. Haig last night was indeed cordial and enjoyable.

Thanks again,
Lou

Sky News

"Harvard started going through one of its spasms of social consciousness by setting up a committee on faculty–student sex last year, so naturally this place had to do the same thing," Amy said. "Their committee issued their finding yesterday. I guarantee you ours will do the same within the month. Eastern State, like a lot of other universities, always decides they must imitate the Ivies. We lesser institutions cannot fall behind when it comes to doing the right thing. Heaven forfend!"

"So Eastern State has decided to outlaw sex between adults?" Mark said.

"Only when it is between innocent, unspoiled undergraduates and lecherous faculty predators," Amy said.

Mark dropped three ice cubes each into a pair of short glasses with weighted bottoms. "It's time for a drink. If we are going to discuss such a weighty matter, I'd better pour the Wild Turkey.

We'll need the extra twenty proof." He poured three fingers for each of them.

"If ESU is going to try to be Harvard, and to create its own version of a perfectly just and socially conscious society," Amy said, "I guess we should define our terms. What is an undergraduate student? What is a faculty member?"

Mark enjoyed the bracing effect of his first swallow of the hundred–proof bourbon. "Spoken like a true faculty predator. An undergraduate student is obviously an eighteen–to–twenty–two-year–old who has come to ESU to sit at the feet of wise, learned, and all too often horny members of the faculty, and who are often dazzled by their erudition. And, those undergraduates apparently are often seduced by said faculty members."

"So what the Hell are you doing here, Sergeant?" Amy said.

Mark did not sip his drink; he preferred healthy swallows. "Why I've come to learn to write a sentence, maybe even a paragraph, so that I can eventually get a bachelor's degree, become a teacher, and train young minds myself. And, if I'm lucky, to be seduced by some worldly professor."

"Bullshit!" You are a retired soldier with a Bronze Star and a Purple Heart. You've published four short stories, and about a dozen poems. That's more than twice as much as several of our creative writing faculty. You intimidate those who don't have tenure. Our female professors don't want to seduce you; they are afraid of you."

"Except for one," Mark said.

Amy chewed on an ice cube. She liked having an old habit that annoyed Mark. "Yes, there is that one."

"Since we're defining terms," Mark said, "how would you define professors, professor?"

"Why we are wise, hard–working, underpaid scholars. We dazzle our students with our vast stores of knowledge. And, of course, many of use the unequal power inherent in faculty–student interactions to take sexual advantage of our students." She cracked an ice cube in half. Mark winced.

"Sounds about right. And your greater age and sophistication add to your authority and your ability to dominate us naïve undergraduates."

"Yeah. You're right," Amy said. "I'm within three days of being fifteen months older than you. That's how I bully you into keeping the house squared away. You have every reason to be afraid of me."

"Another drink?"

"I have to think about it. Do I grade papers tonight, or do I want to continue to discuss Eastern's latest attempt to protect you and your fellow innocents from the likes of me?" She held out her glass. "I've thought about it. Another Wild Turkey, lackey!"

Mark dropped fresh ice cubes into their glasses and picked up the bottle. "You are the professional academic. Isn't this new policy mostly for show, one of those things meant to say 'Eastern State University is a nurturing, supportive institution'? Just another of those bouts of sanctimony that universities like to engage in once in a while?"

"Of course. But that's never the end of it. Every time a university goes into the preachy 'supporting, protecting' mode, some odd or tricky case comes up. There is always some set of circumstances that nobody foresaw or intended the policy to address. That's why so many schools have tied themselves in knots trying to deal with sexual assault cases. They just don't know how to handle them."

"That's for damn sure," Mark said. "Sexual assault is a crime. The cops, the courts, and long sentences should handle it, not well–intentioned history and biology profs and resume–building student politicians. But I have to admit that the Army didn't handle it any better."

"Let's stop with the sarcasm," Amy said, and talk about what, if anything, this means for us."

Mark finished his second drink. "Yeah. You're right. But this kind of sanctimonious do–gooding begs for sarcasm. And we both come from backgrounds that produce expert practitioners. I never thought any institution could match the Army's frequency and expertise in the dark arts of sarcasm. Then I came to a university. I not only met professional academics, but moved in with one. *Then* I learned sarcasm. The Army ought to hire professors as consultants, to teach sarcasm to NCOs and officers."

"You got that right, soldier boy. And we are fighting for the lead in sanctimony, too."

"You are the professional in this place and in this relationship," Mark said. "What does it really mean for us?"

"I'm assuming it means nothing," Amy said. "That we live together is no secret. Everybody in my department knows it. We go to faculty parties together, for Pete's sake."

"Yeah. And nobody has ever given me any crap at those scintillating soirées."

"Watch the sarcasm, Sarge. The men don't give you any crap because they are afraid of you. And the women don't give me any crap because they are jealous. Give me another half a drink. I don't see me grading any papers tonight."

"So you don't see your dean having a problem?" Mark said.

"Not unless somebody forces the issue. I think that in most relationship–related cases—and somebody needs to think of a better term—it is a student who initiates the complaint that gets the machinery moving.

"If I asked you to come upstairs with me, right now, you wouldn't file a complaint, would you?"

"Why Professor, are you using the inherent power imbalance in our relationship to coerce me?"

Amy walked to the staircase. "One more sarcastic remark and I'll withdraw the invitation."

Covering the Spread

In Pigwell, time is not measured by days or weeks but by the number of eighteen wheelers that drive past my house. Our town is on the outskirts of the edge of the world, one hell of a long way from Eastern State University. But I want to graduate from ESU, so I'm taking this course by correspondence.

I live in an old house on the edge of Pigwell that my brother lets me use. It sits on Highway 42, near the crest of a hill. I can hear the westbound truckers downshift coming up the hill. Going east, they accelerate on the downhill grade. I can't swear that I hear every truck; sometimes I go off for a walk in the woods. But I'm pretty sure we get two or three trucks most days. I figure that when I've heard twenty–five or thirty trucks go by it must be Sunday; another week has passed. But I wouldn't swear to it. And it really doesn't matter.

I feel stupid writing stuff like this, but in the course study guide you asked where we live, what else is going on in our lives, and why we are taking this course. Well, it is the only thing I can take from Pigwell. I could take it at the South Pole (almost as isolated as Pigwell) if I wanted to.

In spite of some serious differences that have developed between ESU and me, I've decided I want to graduate, no matter how much the school dislikes the idea. With twelve more credit hours, correspondence or not, they have to give it to me. And I WILL go to Capital City for graduations. I'll march across the stage. Provost Pound will have to hear my name and shake my hand.

So now you have an idea of why I decided to take your History 276 course. I guess the real work starts now. While I'm waiting to hear from you, I'll start on the reading for Unit 2. I'll see if I can still do real work.

Sincerely,
Preston LaFong

February 18, 2005

Dear Mr. LaFong:

You certainly made Pigwell sound remote. But given the structure of correspondence study, there is no reason we cannot establish an effective and efficient instructor–student relationship, based entirely on the written word. Why are you working on a Bachelor of General Studies, rather than a degree with a major? You also raised my curiosity about why you think ESU, or at least Provost Pound, would not want you to graduate. You do not have to share any personal information at all, of course. Nothing about your personal life will have any impact on your course grade.

You are right about Unit 2 being the place where the real work begins. History 276 begins just as the Civil War is ending. Many students find the story of Reconstruction, confusing. But I think the textbook author does a good job of explaining its political, economic, and cultural dimensions. I'll look forward to seeing your work.

Cordially,
Paula Jensen

About March 1, 2005

Dear Ms. Jensen,

Unit 2 is attached.

So I didn't tell you enough last time? I left ESU under a cloud. Provost Pound called me "notorious." In fact, I'm surprised, and a little disappointed, that you haven't heard of me.

I'm working the Bachelor of General Studies because it is the quickest route to graduation, and the only ESU degree I could possibly work on from Pigwell. When I started at ESU, I wanted to get a business degree, but it didn't work out. I had a full–time job (really more than full time). Because of scheduling problems, I couldn't get required business administration courses. I had to take whatever classes I could work around my schedule. I piled up a lot of credits, but they led nowhere.

When I decided to leave Capital City, I had taken well over than three years of basically useless courses. A friend's girlfriend worked in the Continuing Education office. She said I ought to visit the adult student adviser out there to see if there was some way to get the degree. I went to see her (Gail Forrest; she said that you are a good teacher). Gail said in order to get the business degree, I'd have to take two more full years of courses.

But she also had good news. Gail said that with all my liberal arts hours, and just four more courses, I could earn the Bachelor of General Studies. To make it better, I could take all of the courses by correspondence, and thus could get the hell out of Dodge, I had a program and a place that offered solitude. I could still earn the degree, wear the ring, and piss off Provost Pound.

Pigwell has everything I need. I live free at my brother's old house. Thanks to the pork–barrel skills of our congressman—sort of a Robert Byrd of the backwoods—Pigwell has its own post office. It employs one–and–a–half people, making it the largest employer in town (unless you consider the brother and two sisters with the meth lab).

Now, as they say in jokes, "But enough about me. . . ." You were right about Unit 2 and Reconstruction. I hope you'll like my essay.

I guess it's time to get into the dreary politics of the late 1800s—populism, the free coinage of silver, and all that crap.

Sincerely,
Preston LaFong

March 4, 2005

Dear Mr. LaFong,

Your Unit 2 is attached, with my comments in the margins. You shaped your argument well.

You teased me by saying that you were notorious, but didn't have the courtesy to tell me why. I guess I could Google you, but I think I'll just stay curious until you choose to tell me why you are infamous.

It's time to get on with Unit 3. Maybe you'll find it more interesting than you expected. William Jennings Bryan was one of the most passionate, interesting characters in American history, if somewhat odd. And I think you'll like the textbook's speculations on the *Wizard of Oz.*

March 20, 2005 (give or take)

Dear Ms. Jensen,

I appreciated your comments on Unit 2. As far as Unit 3 goes, the assigned readings were better than I had expected, although I still consider Bryan a fraud. The article by Littlefield that interpreted the *Wizard of Oz* as a parable about politics was a treat, but I'm not sure I buy it.

I guess I do owe you an explanation of the "notorious" bomb in my last letter. Maybe next time.

Sincerely,
Preston LaFong

March 26, 2005

Dear Mr. LaFong:

I'm glad you liked the Littlefield article. Ever since it came out, there have been debates about whether L. Frank Baum had carefully crafted an extended critique of capitalism in the age of the robber barons, or if he had just tried to write a lively, entertaining children's book.

You are doing excellent work. Keep it up.

Paula Jensen

Roughly April 4, 2005

Dear Ms. Jensen

My Unit 3 assignment is enclosed. It was a heavy one. I knew almost nothing about American imperialism until I did the assigned readings. The Mark Twain commentary on the Philippines Insurrection surprised me. It was some dark and bitter stuff.

Are you ready for an explanation? I'm living in Pigwell instead of Capital City because almost everybody at ESU thinks I helped fix a football game. The "more–than–fulltime" job I told you about was my athletic scholarship. Playing football created the scheduling problems I complained about. Football coaches don't schedule classes for athletes' convenience. That's why I have such an assortment of courses. I took whatever I could get, whenever I could get it.

After the rumors started, I managed to stick out the rest of the semester. But as soon as it ended, I left school and came to Pigwell. This place is so small and remote that it doesn't even have a restaurant—decent or otherwise—and no bars. There is no way that reporters, NCAA investigators, or F.B.I. agents are going to hang around.

Sincerely,
Preston

April 10, 2005

Dear Mr. LaFong,

I have been teaching this course for almost
ten years, and I've probably had 300 or more
students go through it. Your response to the
question about the critics of imperialism was
among the very best I've seen.

Thank you for telling me about your
"notoriety." I was curious. And you were right; I
have little knowledge of college sports and even
less interest. No wonder I didn't recognize your
name.

I'm afraid my curiosity has gotten the better
of me. You said that people at ESU *believe* you
threw a football game. Did you? You don't have
to answer, of course.

Thanks,
Paula Jensen

April 15, 2005, maybe

Dear Ms. Jensen,

Thank you for the compliment on Unit 4. Units 5 and 6 are enclosed. How could Woodrow Wilson be such an idealist, with genuinely noble ideals, but be so wrong? His unwillingness to compromise undid his plan for a safe, civilized world.

Did I do it? I'll tell you what I told everyone else: I have nothing to say. Why would I want to say something that someone, anyone, might construe as incriminating? Would you say something that might draw a prosecutor to your door, no matter how innocent your remarks might be?

It looks like I'm going to be doing a lot of reading about Franklin Roosevelt.

Next time,
Preston

May 2, 2005

Dear Preston,

As usual, the greatest part of my response to your last two units is scribbled in the margins of your essays.

Woodrow Wilson is a difficult figure. A more cynical and pragmatic politician knows when it's time to make a deal. Actually, you did a good job of showing what can happen to an idealist burdened by a sense of absolute moral certainty.

I understand your reluctance to directly confront the accusations that you cheated in football. I apologize for asking. Without saying anything about the incident in which you were involved, would you mind educating me a little? How does somebody "throw" a football game? Wouldn't the whole team have to be involved?

Sincerely,
Paula Jensen

Must be around May 8, 2005

Dear Ms Jensen:

Units 7 and 8 are attached. My head is still spinning from trying to memorize all of the New Deal agencies. As much as Roosevelt dominated the political landscape, I still don't think I have a real grasp of who he was. He seems to have been unusually accessible on one level and elusive on another. My confusion will be obvious when you read my Unit 7 essays.

Now to *your* education: I'll try to keep it simple. Gamblers establish a "spread," a point margin that hypothetically erases the difference in talent and ability of the two teams. For example, the gamblers might say that Notre Dame is good enough to beat Alabama by 14 points. If I bet on Notre Dame, it would not only have to win, but to win by 14 or more points in order for me to collect the bet. On the other hand, if you bet on Alabama, if it lost by 14 points or less, you would win the bet.

The most common way to throw a game is to try to "shave" points by making mistakes that aren't too obvious, at critical times, so that the favored team will not "cover" the spread. This is not an exact science, of course. Sometimes the "mistakes" are too obvious.

On to the Cold War.

Sincerely,
Preston

May 15, 2005

Dear Preston,

Many people, even some historians, have had the same problem you did in grasping Roosevelt's personality and style. FDR knew that in public policy, compromise was necessary. One biographer subtitled his book *The Lion and the Fox*, which captures both FDR's public style and his secret maneuverings.

Thanks for the information on sports gambling. You're a good teacher.

Sincerely,
Paula Jensen

May 22, 2005, Maybe.

Dear Ms. Jensen,

I appreciate all of the feedback on my essays. Your red ink comments are teaching me a lot. So are the assigned readings.

Unit 9 is one of the most interesting, so far. I guess you are right about FDR. He didn't mind lying. His pro–England actions in 1940–1941 would get a president impeached today. He seems to have been a master of deceit, but for all the right reasons. On the other hand, Truman didn't bother with deception. I liked the textbook's story of the Truman–MacArthur smackdown.

I was not going to do this, but since you are interested, I'll tell you how my troubles got started. In the 2003 Copper Bowl, ESU was favored to beat Western Tech; the spread was 10 points. On the opening kickoff, our All–American running back, Ronnie Hunt, fumbled. Tech recovered, and drove for a touchdown. Things just got worse after that. Ronnie fumbled three more times.

I was a defensive player, a cornerback. It was my job to break up pass plays. Tech put in a freshman wide receiver that they had hardly used all season, due to injuries and disciplinary problems. He turned out to be half–a–step faster than anyone else I had ever covered; that was all it took. He burned me on four long plays, once for a touchdown.

Not only didn't we cover the spread, we were slaughtered. The Capital City papers found the loss embarrassing. A columnist "wondered" if there could be some explanation other than the relative talent of the two teams. People started saying things like, "You can't tell me that Hunt fumbling four times was an accident. He only fumbled once the whole season." And, "A freshman wide receiver burned LaFong over and over? You *know* that's not right." So that's how it started.

Sincerely,
Preston

June 1, 2005

Dear Preston,

Thanks for the nice words about the course. Many students find the frequent red marks intimidating. You are doing extremely well. You have the writing skills and self discipline needed for success in correspondence study.

You really surprised me by revealing so much about the game that seems to have damaged your education, and if I may say so, your life. Thank you.

Thanks,
Paula

It could be June 10, 2005

Dear Ms. Jensen:

McCarthyism was the most interesting thing covered in Unit 10. I can understand how Arthur Miller used it as the inspiration for the witch hunt in *The Crucible*. I'd like to see it some day.

The suspicion about whether Ronnie and I threw a game is not going to ruin my life. I wouldn't be taking this course from you if I wasn't determined to move on.

Remember, no one has found any evidence implicating either Ronnie Hunt or me. No district attorney or federal prosecutor came even close to filing a case. The NCAA found no proof of point shaving. ESU has no grounds for suspending or expelling me. But the people there made life extremely unpleasant. They think I betrayed the team. Some of them lost money betting on us.

During the last semester I spent there, those professors who hated sports anyhow liked to point to me as an inevitable example of having a football program. One polit–prof even added me to his "what's wrong with this university" rant.

Provost Pound called me in. He conceded that it didn't look like I would be charged with a crime. Nevertheless, I had nevertheless damaged the name of the University, he said. While I had been duly admitted, he said, it seemed unlikely that I could ever graduate. He clearly meant this as a threat. He warned me that many of the faculty had already decided that I could not meet their standards. I was a marked man. I took the hint and left campus, as he wanted. But he forgot about the BGS, if he had ever even heard about it.

You can go through the BGS and hardly be noticed. Most of the instructors are either teaching assistants or—like you—part–time. Only my adviser Gail keeps track of me. And because correspondence courses don't operate on the semester system, there is no automatic transcript at the close of each semester. The people who run the correspondence program know I'm taking courses, but they don't mind. Besides, nobody ever listens to them. My name will not be noticed until Gail certifies me for graduation. Provost Pound will have no indication of my existence until I am named publicly, in his presence, as a graduate of Eastern State. And then, I'll talk with the reporters I've been avoiding. Pound's bad day will get worse.

In the meantime, I'm in exile in Pigwell, taking courses by myself, one at a time. I'm not counting class days or semester hours, but using eighteen–wheelers as my calendar. Hundreds of them will go by before I finish my four correspondence courses. By the time I serve up revenge at ESU, the dish will be very, very cold— and thus satisfying. Thank you for your help in preparing it.

Sincerely,
Preston

At Alice's

Arlo Guthrie's "talking blues" song "Alice's Restaurant" got the whole country laughing in the late 1960s. It was an eighteen–minute narrative about a young man who was rejected by the draft board because of an old charge of littering. Guthrie's lyrics and delivery were hilarious. But I never laughed as hard at this song as my friends did. Another story about another Alice's Restaurant got in the way.

In my second year at Eastern State University, in Capital City, I had a job as a dormitory proctor. "Proctor" is now an archaic word on campuses. People who do this work are now usually called "resident assistants." They work not in dormitories, but in "residence halls." And nowadays you would never see sophomores in these jobs. Then we did not pretend to be "role models," leading freshmen through "developmental tasks." Our entire job was to maintain a modicum of peace and quiet in the dorms for about twelve hours of the day.

Early on a spring Saturday afternoon Alan, a good friend and fellow proctor walked into my room. He reached over to my radio and turned off the Braves game without asking, which was unlike him. "What's up?" I asked.

"You know Chris, the guy in the room to my left?" he said. "He called me from downtown. He's trapped in Alice's Restaurant with a couple of other freshmen."

"What do you mean, 'trapped'?" Chris, a bright kid from Avalon, New Jersey, had been nothing but trouble since arriving in Capital City at the beginning of the year. He didn't understand—or care about—southern conventions. He enjoyed shooting off his mouth about how backwards southerners were. And of course he wasn't all wrong. But he couldn't seem to learn that insulting the locals, especially off–campus, was a good way to get his ass kicked. He had just narrowly avoided real trouble several times.

Alan sighed. "He and his friends were apparently trying to top each other in telling stories about the locals they had encountered."

"And they chose Alice's to do this in? Why'd they go there, of all places? Not only is it a fatback, overcooked greens, and sweetened tea place," I said, "it's always full of rednecks."

Alan rolled his eyes. "Who knows?"

"So what has that son of the Jersey Shore done?"

He reached for my pack of L&Ms, shook one out, and lighted it. At least he used his own lighter. "Chris must have gotten a little enthusiastic in his description of some of our local citizens. Apparently words like 'shit kickers' and 'peckerwoods' were bandied about. A party of four at a nearby table just happened to be genuine peckerwoods, and apparently proud of it. One of them, in a low—but apparently compelling—voice, asked our boys if they had ever heard about the Klan."

"Oh Hell!"

Alan continued, "He told them to finish their 'dinner,' then they could all go outside and 'talk about manners with you pissants.'"

"That's obviously something we didn't succeed at," I said.

"It got worse. The kluker that was doing the talking opened up his hand to show Chris a small box cutter, the kind with a single–edge razor blade. Because of the other people in the place, the klukers couldn't stop Chris from getting to the payphone. So he called me for help."

"Shouldn't we just call the police?"

"Depending on who we got, that might not turn out too well," said Alan. "I figured maybe we could get a couple of more guys and just go in and walk our guys out."

I thought about it for a moment. "Sounds risky. But if worst comes to worst, it would be eight of us against four of them. Who else is around here today?"

Alan said, "Chuck is in the office. If Kent is in his room that ought to be enough." Neither of them turned us down, although they looked as if they'd like to. We got into Alan's car for the short drive—less than five blocks—to Broadway and Alice's.

"When we get there," Alan said, "we'll walk directly to our boys' table, then walk and talk them out. Once we get our guys moving, we don't stop. We may have to slow down, but we've got to keep moving. And that will be even more important once we get to the sidewalk. If you have to talk to any of the klukers, try to smile and be polite. We'll say we are taking them over to Dean Boggs, who is in his office, ready to talk with our boys about southern manners, and maybe to hand out some punishment. But we keep moving until they are in the car and I can back out. Then the three of you can walk over to the Fain Hall parking lot and I'll meet you there."

The problem was apparent as soon as we walked into Alice's. Chris and his three friends were seated at a table in a back corner of the dining room. All were pale. Closer to the front door sat three men with deep tans. One wore jeans and a sweatshirt, two bib overalls. A fourth man, in khaki work clothes was leaning on the back wall, next to the pay phone. We walked back to our four freshmen.

"Have you paid your tab?" Alan asked. They nodded in the affirmative.

"Leave a bigger tip," I said, hoping that a show of respect for the hard–working waitress might help mollify, or even impress, the critics of our boys' behavior. The four pulled out a few singles and added them to the small pile in the middle of the table.

As soon as the four freshmen stood up, the table of offended southern gentlemen rose quickly and walked toward us. "Those boys need a little learning," said the smallest of them, the man in jeans, who looked more like a ferret than anyone I had ever encountered.

"We're from the Dean of Men's office. The police called and told us to get this bunch out of here before there was any trouble," Alan said. We pulled out our flimsy pasteboard ID cards. Nobody examined them. "Did these boys sass you?"

"Damn straight," said ferret–face, obviously their leader.

"We try to teach them good manners, but they grew up in a strange place where manners aren't valued," I said. "We're about to take these boys over for a talk with Dean Boggs. If he doesn't just throw them out, he'll hand out some pretty tough punishment. He doesn't like kids coming down and insulting the people who live here." This was all a bluff. Nobody had called Boggs. But such was his reputation around Capital City that we hoped our story sounded credible.

We got our boys up and moving and kept them moving. The man in khaki work clothes said, "These boys was really asking for it. He, too, showed us a box cutter. But we kept moving. Once we got out the door and onto the sidewalk the klukers moved even closer in. Their language coarsened.

Alan and I continued our defenders of the Old South act. It was no damn fun having to ride herd on ignorant Yankees who just didn't understand southern ways, especially southern manners. Two more knives were shown surreptitiously, but not brandished. Fortunately the sidewalk was open to view and people were in eyeshot from three directions. Alan opened his car. We shielded the freshmen and pushed them into it. "We'll meet you at Dean Boggs's office," I said. Alan backed out into traffic and headed for the building known informally as the Administration Building (its official name was the Academic Building).

Kent, Chuck, and I headed across the Broadway, onto the campus, then to the parking lot behind Fain Hall. By then Alan had already let the freshmen out, suggesting they not patronize Alice's Restaurant for a couple of years, and that they go somewhere and relax. That was good advice for us, too. We were still shaking.

"Well, those boys learned something about life in the South today," I said.

Alan took a long drag on his Marlboro, exhaled, then said. "Yeah. And it's a damned shame."

I never did learn to enjoy Arlo Guthrie's rendition of "Alice's Restaurant."

Salty Waters

Yankee Station: On the Line

The Navy fixed Yankee Station at 17° 30'N, 108° 30' E, off Vietnam, in the shallowest corner of the Tonkin Gulf. For nine years, American aircraft carriers, three at a time, worked thirty-five straight days on the line, sometimes forty. Twelve hours at flight quarters, twelve hours off. Machinery howled. So did minds.

On each carrier, crewmen armed and fueled Phantoms, Intruders, and Corsairs. They made ready their catapults, arresting gear, and fire-fighting equipment. Men in yellow, green, purple, red, brown, and blue shirts and caps performed a frantic ballet, their steps complicated, swift, dangerous, and—finally—futile.

Obstacle Number Three

Captain Arthur Lemmon, Commanding Officer of the Naval Officer Candidate School (NAVOCS), stared out his office window across the parade grounds, known as the "grinder," supposedly because the officer candidates ground the soles off their shoes there, practicing close–order drill. Lemmon's command was centered on Coddington Point, which protrudes into Narragansett Bay, just north of Newport, Rhode Island. In spite of a brisk wind, there were no whitecaps. The sky was clear and the Bay was a deep, rippled blue, but Captain Lemmon was in a foul mood. His secretary stepped to the door and said, "Lieutenant Horvatic is here."

"Come in, Mr. Horvatic. Take a seat. I hear we have a problem on our hands," Lemmon said.

"I imagine you mean Officer Candidate Joshua Carter, sir," said Lieutenant Horvatic.

"Correct, Mr. Horvatic. I understand that with only two weeks until this class graduates, we may have to wash out the officer candidate who is first in his class—in effect, our valedictorian.

Horvatic didn't like the way the conversation was going. It was too formal, which usually meant trouble. He carefully placed his officer's hat on the coffee table. "Yes, sir. There's a good chance that will happen."

"Run it down for me," the Captain said.

"Yes, sir. Mr. Carter stands at number two in Seamanship, short of number one by just a hair. He is number one, by a wide margin, in both Tactics and Naval Organization. He has been a section leader in Alfa Company, and he's now the student company commander, so his leadership marks are high. He has never seen a red gig," Horvatic said, referring to the OCS equivalent of demerits.

"So why the hell are we going to wash him out?"

"It's the obstacle course, sir," Lieutenant Horvatic said. "Specifically Obstacle Number Three."

Captain Lemmon opened an elaborately carved monkeypod cigarette box he had brought back from the Philippines. He offered the box to Horvatic, who took a Pall Mall. Lemmon then took one. The two men lit up with Horvatic's Zippo lighter, a simple act that reduced the tension and degree of formality in the Captain's office.

"So it's that damned wall?" the CO said.

"Yes, sir. Mr. Carter just can't get over it. While he's shorter than the average officer candidate, he's above the height requirement. And much shorter men make it over the wall all the time."

"So what the hell is the problem, Mike?"

Horvatic used a couple of puffs on his Pall Mall to stall. "Well, he's pear–shaped, sir. Low center of gravity. But he still should have gotten over Number Three by now. I think the problem is in his head."

Captain Lemmon stubbed out his smoke. "So we have to wash him out? You have to know how embarrassing that would be to this command."

"Those are the rules, sir. All officer candidates must run the obstacle course in under fifteen minutes, successfully negotiating each obstacle. Every training company runs the course every week, so they get plenty of tries. Most men are running the course successfully in under ten minutes by their third or fourth try."

"So how many men do we lose this way?" said Lemmon.

"It's rare, sir. I checked. It has been two years since we washed out anybody for O course problems. The previous time was three years before that."

Captain Lemmon stood up. He abruptly

dropped his informal tone. "So what's your feeling on this? Are we going to have the embarrassment of washing out our first–in–class?"

Horvatic began to tense up. "It's sad, sir. He's a natural leader, a real trick for a short man. The Navy will lose a good officer who could have gone far. And since the grade tabulations will be final before the last run at the O course, we probably will have to wash out our top student. But standards are standards. All the other OCs have had to meet them."

"Yeah," Lemmon said. "But that won't satisfy the Navy. It will still demand two years of enlisted service from Carter. It will make him a mess cook on some destroyer or oiler. He'll sling chow and swab decks twelve hours a day." After a long pause, Lemmon continued. "To make it worse, his father is a congressman. Did you know that? He's from some district in southern California. And he is planning to come here for graduation. Somebody from the Pentagon, from BUSHIPS, called last week to let me know Carter's father is on the appropriations subcommittee that will be looking at the 1968–1972 shipbuilding appropriation. It's not going to be fun to tell him his boy couldn't hack it here, so he will be peeling potatoes for a couple of years. What am I going to say? Maybe I could say, 'At least it will keep him from getting drafted'."

Horvatic knew that senior officers like Lemmon did not like to be sent to training commands. While NAVOCS was among the better training commands, it was by no means considered a prestigious rung on the career ladder. It was more of a side step. With any missteps or political messes, his next assignment would probably be a dead end job that would end his dwindling hopes for an admiral's star.

"You are the Alfa Company Officer," Captain Lemmon said. "Do you have a problem running your unit? Do the student officers in your company not give a damn about their classmates?"

Horvatic could see that the Captain intended to load the blame for Carter's misfortunes on his desk. *It's the same old story: shit rolls downhill.* "No, sir," he said. Our student company commander, Officer Candidate Rice, is among the best, like Carter. He is a natural leader. And the others are good, also."

"Then why the Hell are they not giving Mr. Carter some help getting over that wall? Helping your brother OC get through this place is one of the things we're supposed to be teaching. I suggest that you have a talk with your student officers, soon."

At Newport, as in all U.S. military officer training institutions, most of the real work of the day–to–day supervision of officer candidates is done by student officers, not by the professional officers in charge of the school. The professional officers select the student officers, based on their performance and the recommendations of the student officers from preceding classes.

Immediately upon returning to his office, Lieutenant Horvatic summoned his student Company Commander, Leonard Rice. "Mr. Rice, what have you and the other Alfa Company student officers done to help Mr. Carter get across Obstacle Three? Rice stood at parade rest, hands clasped behind his back. Horvatic did not say "at ease." He never considered inviting Rice to smoke, of course.

"We have taken him out to the O course after lights out twice, to try to help him with his technique. And several times, a couple of guys have given up their Saturday afternoon or Sunday morning liberty to work with him. He tries like hell, but he's never gotten over a single time. He appears to give it all he has, but he just chokes. Every one of us wants to see him top that wall."

"You better see that he does!" snapped Horvatic. It sounds to me like you and your other student officers may need some Extra Military Instruction. Maybe Thursday night. Dismissed." Rice left quickly and quietly, wondering what kind of misfortune Lieutenant Horvatic might dream up.

That evening, in the brief period between mess and study hours, Len Rice called a meeting with two of Alfa Company's section leaders. "It's time to get serious about getting Josh over that damned wall. He's got one more chance." He told them about his meeting with Lieutenant Horvatic. "He said *we* might need some Extra Military Instruction, instead of liberty, on the night before graduation."

"But my wife and I have big plans," said the older section leader.

"Everybody has big plans for that night," Rice said. "This, gentlemen, is a good lesson in what rolls downhill. Josh has one more chance. Alfa Company is scheduled for the O course on Wednesday morning. You two will run the course just ahead of him. When you get over the wall, stay close to it so that you can report to me that he got over in good form."

"In good form!" the younger section leader said. Form doesn't matter. You just have to get over."

Rice continued, "I have to sign off if he successfully gets over. But I have to watch from the front side of the wall, so I can make sure his takeoff is valid. So I won't be able to see his landing."

"You're nuts!" said the younger section leader. "None of that matters. Nobody scores form."

Rice stared, hard, at the older section leader, who stared back, After a long pause, he suddenly smiled slightly, then said, "I understand."

On Wednesday morning of graduation week, Alfa Company lined up for its last try at the obstacle course. The OCs tried not to look at Josh Carter. Nonetheless, he was the center of attention. Everyone knew that tonight he would either join the company party downtown at Vesuvio's, or be sitting in the transit barracks, waiting for orders to report to a ship for two years' enlisted service.

Student Company Commander Rice ordered his men into single file, then stepped in behind Carter. The two section leaders were directly in front of him. The first man in line took off, jumped a set of four hurdles, hopscotched through the double line of tires, then ran to Obstacle Three. He extended his left leg toward it and let his momentum carry him forward and up. He grabbed the top, and swung over. So did the second, third, and fourth men, then the two section leaders.

Officer Candidate Joshua Carter had begun that morning with an extended trip to the head, followed by several more, shorter trips. Since getting into his athletic gear, he had been able to think of nothing beyond cleaning grease traps in a galley on a ship in the North Atlantic.

Carter began his run. He hit the obstacle with his left foot, but a little low. Rice saw him pull himself up enough to get both arms across the top. Then, suddenly, he was over. Rice followed, hit the wall and rolled over. Carter was struggling to stand up.

The younger section leader said, "He fell hard, right on his face and chest. But he looks okay."

"Maybe a little stunned," said Rice. Men kept coming over the wall, doing their best to stay clear of Carter, Rice, and the two section leaders as they headed for Obstacle Four.

Rice and the section leaders got Carter to his feet and pointed him in the right direction. He moved slowly at first, but managed to come in more than two minutes under the allotted fifteen. By the time Carter got to the finish line, Rice had already signed his satisfactory completion form. He pounded him on the back and said, "You're an officer now; first in your class! Drinks are on you tonight."

On the far side of the parking lot adjacent to the course, Captain Lemmon and Lieutenant Horvatic, hats removed, in semi–crouches, peered across the top of a Pontiac and watched the finish line celebration. "Well, Mike, your boys finally learned something about standing with their shipmates," the Captain said. "They just *snatched* our number one in his class across that wall, damned sure that nobody saw them. They learned that shit is not the only thing that rolls downhill. So does leadership." He reached into his left sock and pulled out a pack of Pall Malls. "Smoke 'em if you got 'em, Mike."

Laundry Bag: Green, Nylon

> For every Southern boy fourteen years
> old, not once, but whenever he wants it,
> there is the instant when it's still not yet
> two o'clock on that July afternoon in 1863,
> the brigades are in position behind the rail
> fence, the guns are laid and ready in the
> woods . . . it hasn't happened yet, . . .
>
> —William Faulkner
> *Intruder in the Dust*

The 1MC loudspeaker sounded "Mail Call" while
Ensign Mills was Engineering Watch Officer
in Main Engine Control. When LTJG Garvey
relieved him at 1630, Mills ascended four decks,
walked forward fifteen feet, and entered the
Engineering Log Room to check his mail slot. The
news was waiting for him in a plain white envelope
addressed in Frankie's loopy handwriting.

Mills and the *Mariana Straits* (CVA-44) had been in WESTPAC—mainly the Tonkin Gulf—for five months. One of the Navy's oldest aircraft carriers, the *Mariana Straits* provided a platform for bombing attacks on North Vietnam and Laos. Over the deployment, Frankie's letters had become progressively less personal and affectionate. To Mills, they read like vague messages sent mainly out of a sense of obligation. Then—two months ago—Mills started picking up indications that another man had entered the picture. Just two weeks earlier, he had received two letters, a day apart, telling him it was all over but the shouting.

He sent a pathetic letter, asking her not to make any sudden decisions, to at least wait until the ship made a port call, so that he could phone and talk things out. Hopeful that she might change her mind, he knew better. While aware of the futility of this line of thought, he could not jettison it.

Mills walked forward to the Auxiliaries, or "A" Division office. As usual at 1630, his boss and the two enlisted men he shared it with were gone. He lighted a Benson and Hedges and opened the letter with an electrician's knife from his desk. This was it—the full, classic "Dear John" that military men have received since the advent of postal service.

Frankie closed with, "I hope you will not let yourself become bitter."

Mills snuffed out his smoke, stared at the sickly green bulkhead, then lighted another cigarette. He finally picked up a lined pad and a government–issue ballpoint. "I *am* bitter. You can tell me to get out of your life, to get lost, but you can't tell me how to feel. Remembering the last five miserable months should help me stay bitter for a long time. Please destroy my letters." As if she hadn't already. "Good–bye."

Mills did not wish her happiness or good fortune with her new man. He did not bother to sign the note. Starting now, he wanted to waste as little time as possible on Frankie. But he knew himself. He would waste many hours—especially on dull night watches—replaying events, conversations, and letters in his head.

At first, he hoped his abrupt, defiant, and surly tone would feel satisfying. It didn't. And now, even though nobody on the ship knew—or ever needed to know—anything about it, he nonetheless felt humiliated. But the anger felt better than the anxiety and depression he had been living with.

He found a plain "civilian" envelope, inserted and sealed his unsigned message into it, addressed it, and wrote "free" on the top right corner. It was one of the "benefits" of serving in a war zone.

As his roommate Steve liked to sardonically say when junior officers gathered to complain, "The free postage makes it all worthwhile."

On his way aft to the wardroom, Mills dropped the letter into the slot of a locked box mounted outside the ship's post office. During evening mess he refrained from the usual banter with the other junior officers. He decided to watch the wardroom movie at 1900. He was in luck. It was Clint Eastwood in *The Good, The Bad, and The Ugly*. The film's action and violence precluded self–absorption and reflection. This alone ensured that it would become a shipboard favorite.

After the movie, Mills quickly showered and headed for his rack. At least he didn't worry about losing sleep because of Frankie. Sleep deprivation is a constant at sea. Sailors go into a deep sleep quickly at any opportunity. With the exception of a few carrier captains worried about making admiral, there were no insomniacs in the Tonkin Gulf.

Mills stood the eight to twelve (0730–1130) Main Engine Control watch the next day. With flight operations underway, it was a busy watch, with numerous speed changes and log entries. In calm weather every launch cycle meant putting on flank speed to make 33 knots across the deck, the wind speed necessary to launch the Phantoms, Intruders, and Corsairs. Every piece of machinery in Main Control seemed to vibrate and rattle any time the *Mariana Straits* hit 30 knots. Still, between launches, Frankie made her appearance. He did his best to squelch the shadow of anger and sense of betrayal, but could not pull it off.

Being pissed off was not enough. Mills was from South Carolina, home of the "fire eaters," the most strident proponents of secession from the Union. He had long since dropped any nostalgia about the Civil War and the Old South. In fact, he considered himself to the left of center, politically. However, as Faulkner said of every Southern boy, he retained the visceral, romantic sense of a lost cause. In the face of certain defeat, Faulkner's boy—and grown men like Mills— could at any time summon up that instant at Gettysburg, just before two o'clock on July 3, 1863, the seconds before General James Longstreet gave George Pickett and two other generals the order to advance toward the Union position on Cemetery Ridge. At that moment, possibility still existed. However, with Longstreet's order, came the certainty of decisive defeat.

Like other southern boys, Mills intuitively knew he had to respond to defeat with a grand, romantic, and utterly futile gesture. And he knew he must do it with full knowledge of its futility.

LTJG Garvey relieved Mills at precisely 1130. He walked aft and stopped at Ship's Store #3, in Officers' Country. He asked for two cartons of Benson and Hedges and handed over three one–dollar bills. The storekeeper returned two dimes.

On impulse, Mills said, "Let me have a laundry bag," and handed over another single. In his stateroom, he removed the bag's label— "Laundry bag: green, nylon." It was an open–weave cord bag, with a drawstring closure. Everyone on board used them to turn over their dirty uniforms, underwear, and socks to the ship's laundry. Because of their open weave, they could be stretched to hold an amazing amount of dirty clothes.

All officers' staterooms had small safes built into their drop–front desks. Mills opened his safe and pulled out the stationery box that held Frankie's letters. He dumped them into the bag, then threw the box in for good measure. He added a small photo album without pausing for a last look. The five–by–eight close–up of Frankie on his desk, a shot he had taken himself, went into the bag, frame and all. On the last trip home, Frankie had given him two books, a mystery and a collection of poetry. Into the bag. Finally, he took an oxford–cloth shirt, a pair of red silk boxer shorts, and a silver key ring out of his locker and deposited them in the green bag.

The executive officer constantly reminded the crew not to throw loose paper overboard. A Russian trawler shadowed every carrier task force. Their crews pretended to fish, but everyone knew their job was to observe everything about carrier operations in the South China Sea, particularly in the Tonkin Gulf. If they had a chance, they liked to scoop up loose papers before they became waterlogged and sank.

According to the XO, even such seemingly innocuous documents as the plan of the day could give the Soviets useful data. Thus, documents were to be shredded or disposed of in closed containers, an instruction that was frequently disregarded. On rare occasions, one of the picket destroyers accompanying the carriers had snagged loose pieces of paper and returned them to embarrassed—and furious—carrier captains. "Brown shoe" carrier skippers hated nothing more than being shown up by "black shoe" destroyer skippers.

In reality, Mills wasn't worried about having Frankie's letters fall into the hands of a Russian sailor or an American destroyer crew. The chances of either were remote. Instead, it was the gesture—romantic and pointless—that mattered. He could not say a gracious or graceful farewell. He did not want to quietly dispose of the physical reminders of Frankie. He wanted to eradicate the letters, to send them to the bottom at flank speed.

Mills took a ladder up to the hangar deck. The officer in charge of Repair 1 Alfa in emergency situations, he had a key to its repair locker, a secured space where firefighting and damage control equipment was stored. He unlocked the door, and looked around. He dropped a dogging wrench—a length of pipe used to open and close watertight doors—and a cast iron y–valve into the green nylon bag, thereby adding about ten pounds to its weight. He stepped out of the locker, secured it, and slung the green nylon bag over his shoulder. It had a satisfying heft; it would do.

On the old carriers, a bulkhead separates the hangar deck from the fantail. The fantail is at the stern, open to the air, but sheltered by the last few yards of the flight deck directly overhead. Mills stepped through the open door onto the fantail. Because it was the only part of the hangar deck where the smoking lamp was ever lighted, a few sailors always stood there, silent, smoking, staring out to the horizon.

The trash chute was mounted on the outside of the starboard rail. Mills did not hesitate. He swung the green bag around and dropped it. The cast–iron valve and the dogging wrench clanged against the inside of the chute. The letters and pictures began to decompose before the bag hit the bottom, only about 200 feet in this part of the Gulf. The voice was faint, but firm. "General Pickett, commence moving out your men."

Flank Speed

"Good morning, Bob. Ensign Tim Ryder and I are here—ready, fit, and eager to take the watch. We will bring added glory to the USS Mariana Straits, the noblest carrier in the fleet, and strike fear into the hearts of North Vietnamese forces everywhere."

"Good morning, Bill. Tim, too bad you have to spend your first Assistant Engineering Officer of the Watch duty with our hilarious Mr. Carson. In a few weeks you can start standing your watches with serious engineers. In another couple of months you will qualify as Engineering Officer of the Watch yourself."

"Don't you want breakfast, Bob? Let's get on with the show! I am ready to relieve you, Sir."

"I am ready to be relieved. At 0730, 3 April 1969, we are steaming at eighteen knots. All four main engines are on line, on eight boilers, split four ways. Chief Machinist's Mate Rice is relieving Chief Boilerman Phelps as Chief of the Watch, as we speak.

Flight quarters commenced at 0600, with the first launch at 0630. The next launch–recovery cycle is scheduled for 0800."

"Anything else?"

"The Bridge says there will be no wind at all today. We are going to have to make thirty–three knots in order to put enough wind across the deck to launch and recover aircraft. The Officer of the Deck was as nervous as a cat during the first launch. He called us constantly to check our readiness to make and maintain flank speed."

"Did he use the phone or the 2–MC?"

"The squawk box."

"Shit. That means everybody up on the Bridge and down here in Main Control can hear every word of the bitching and moaning."

"Okay, Bob. Enjoy your breakfast. And most importantly, I relieve you, Sir."

"I stand relieved. Mr. Carson has the watch."

"I hope you noticed the formal language, Tim. The watch is officially changed only when the off–going officer announces to everyone in Main Control that the oncoming officer has the watch. Bob obviously had a rough watch. The engines and boilers on this barge were built just after World War II to launch propeller–driven planes. But the F–4 Phantoms and A–6 Intruders we launch now are the finest, most modern carrier aircraft in existence. In short, an ancient ship with an obsolete propulsion system has to launch state–of–the–art jet aircraft. It's a real mismatch in technology. Now, let's start making an Engineering Officer of the Watch out of you.

"This is the 2–MC, the squawk box. You've seen it in World War II movies. When the Bridge calls down, you and everybody else in Main Engine Control will hear what the OOD says. When you answer, remember that the Captain may be standing right there with him, listening to you.

"When you hear 'Main Control, Bridge,' press down the second switch and say 'Main Control, aye,' then let up on it. The OOD will tell you something, or ask you something. If it is just information, or a simple order, press down on the switch again and say, 'Main Control, aye,' then let up on the switch. Give them what they want and hope that's the end of it."

"It sounds like you don't like to hear from the Bridge, Bill."

"You will learn that the less you can communicate with the Bridge, the better your watch. And whenever we can, we try to use the ordinary phones. They make for clearer and less officious communications.

"Over our next few watches, I'll teach you how to keep the Main Engine Control log. Most of what we write is formula, boilerplate. But if something goes wrong, you want to make sure our side of it is thoroughly documented. If there should be a major equipment failure, for example, make sure that any warning of it, its consequences, and its resolution are recorded. A clean, concise listing of events, as they happened, will minimize the opportunity for anyone else to shift blame to us, meaning you and me.

"Don't take shortcuts with the log. If you make a mistake, draw a line through it, initial it, then write in the correction. You are allowed only two line–outs per page. If you make a third error, go back and rewrite the whole page. It is a pain in the butt, of course. But If you leave an inaccurate statement in there just because you don't want to rewrite the page, it could come back to haunt you."

"Why is everybody so afraid of making a mistake all the time?"

"Tim, have you ever heard the old Navy saying, 'Somebody's got to hang?'"

"Only as black humor."

"When it's your ass in a sling, black humor isn't funny. There's nothing I can teach you that's more important than covering your ass. And the log is the most critical tool for doing so."

"Okay."

"Chief Rice, can you step over here for a minute? This is Mr. Ryder. He came aboard in

Subic Bay. Mr. Ryder, Chief Rice knows this
ship's steam plant nut–by–nut, bolt–by–bolt.
When you've got a machinery problem, and
especially when the Bridge is aware of it, get the
Chief of the Watch on it right away. If you are
lucky, Chief Rice will be on watch. But all the
other chiefs are nearly as good."

"Welcome aboard, Sir. But, the other chiefs
aren't nearly as good as I am."

"Good to meet you, Chief."

"Main Control, Bridge."

"Let me take the squawk box, Tim."

"Main Control, aye."

"Main Control, in about fifteen minutes we
will signal flank speed and order you to make
turns for thirty–five knots. We wanted to give
you a warning."

"Bridge, the Mariana Straits has never made
thirty–five knots. Thirty–three knots, in fact, is
the ship's record."

"Main Control, the Captain wants thirty–five
knots. The A–6's are launching heavy today."

"Main Control, this is the Captain. Who's
EOOW?"

"Bridge, this is Lieutenant Junior Grade
William Carson, Engineering Officer of the
Watch. Good morning, Captain."

"Bill, the 0830 launch is critical to the ship's
mission. The weather is dead calm. Our Intruders

are loaded to the max. Some of them struggled during the 0630 launch. They need more wind under their wings. When the OOD signals All Ahead Flank, open the throttles all the way! I understand that thirty–five knots will be ship's record. You will have the honor of entering it in the engineering log. Am I clear?"

"Yes, Sir. Main Control, aye."

"Chief, you heard the Captain. Do you think that we can make thirty–five knots in this antique? And more importantly, can we sustain it for twenty to twenty–five minutes?"

"Probably, Sir. But it will be with a really heavy fuel mixture that will put a lot of thick, black smoke in the groove. That shouldn't matter while launching, but we will have to clear it immediately in order to commence recovery of the returning aircraft from the 0630 launch. Also, there will be an increased chance of engine overheating."

"Thanks, Chief. If the Bridge wants the knots, it'll have to take the black smoke."

"Aye, aye, Sir."

"Tim, 'the groove' is the approach pathway. Landing pilots must have a clear vision of the flight deck. We are trying for a new ship's record! If we make it, the Captain and the Air Group Commander will be happy, for about a day. But then, when the Admiral—he's over on the Ticonderoga—starts bitching about the black smoke he's been seeing from the Mariana Straits, the CO will catch shit for it, and that commodity always rolls downhill. So, what do you think the next step is?"

"A log entry noting the Captain's request?"

"First, it wasn't a request; it was an order. However, we can't say something like 'the C.O. ordered Main Control to disregard black smoke.' If I put that in the log, the C.O. would confine me to the ship for the rest of the deployment. Our next step is to call our boss, Commander Jones, the Chief Engineer. We need to put him between us and the Captain. The more people who outrank us who know about this order for risky speed, the better."

"I swear Bill, everybody seems to spend more time figuring out who has told who what, and trying to dodge blame, than in actually moving the ship."

"Now you're beginning to understand the carrier Navy, Tim. Look at the compass repeater; it's about two feet above the 3 Engine throttle valve. You can see that the OOD is turning the ship into the wind. And those bells were the engine order telegraph. The OOD has ordered flank speed, with turns for thirty–five knots, as he said he would ten minutes ago.

"Here we go, Tim. We are making turns for thirty–four knots and moving up to thirty–five, a new ship's record."

"Sir, Number 2 Engine reports a hot bearing. It's up to 174 degrees."

"A hot bearing already, Chief? And we've been making flank speed for less than five minutes. Tell the 2 Engine Top Watch to start draping wet towels over the bearing, and to give us a reading every minute."

"I already did, Sir. Not that it will do any good."

"I know, Chief. But it will look good in the log.

"Bridge, Main Control. We have a hot bearing in 2 Engine, 174 degrees and rising. We've implemented emergency cooling measures."

"Main Control, this is the Captain! Bill, this is critical. Can you get that bearing under control, or am I going to have to scrub the launch?"

"Sir, I've called the Chief Engineer. Commander Jones is going down to 2 Engine to take a look at the bearing himself."

"Bill, I don't have time for that. Six aircraft have started their engines. The others are right behind them. Jets don't idle. We are going to have to get them airborne within a couple of minutes or shut them down. And I've got twelve planes from the 0630 launch lining up for recovery. How much of a risk will we be taking by keeping the ship at flank speed for another thirty minutes?"

"Flank speed is meant for only emergency maneuvering, Captain. When we sustain flank speed, we risk overheating engines. A hot bearing can take the whole engine down."

"Dammit, Mr. Carson, I know that. Don't talk to me like I'm some ensign. And stop being chickenshit! Can you keep that bearing under control, or do I scrub this launch right now?"

"Under the circumstances, Captain, I recommend scrubbing the launch. If the bearing temperature continues to rise, we will probably have to take Number 2 Engine out of commission."

"Main Control, Bridge. Commander Jones just called us directly from 2 Engine. He believes that the bearing temperature has crested. The Captain has given the order to launch. Maintain flank speed; continue making turns for 35 knots."

"Main Control, aye. But let us know the second the last plane goes off. We'll need to clear the smoke asap to recover the aircraft from the 0630 launch."

"Bridge, aye."

"Well Chief, it looks like we will either set the speed record for this old scow or come to a sudden stop."

"Yes, Sir."

"Tim, watch me closely. I'm going to log in every report of bearing temperature, every warning, and every caution we gave the OOD, the Captain, and Commander Jones, along with their responses and orders. We are putting extreme demands on the engines. The 2 Engine bearing may yet fail. In case it does, my recommendation to scrub the launch has to be in the log, along with Commander Jones's okay on the bearing and the C.O.'s decision to launch. You are going to learn how to cover your ass from a master."

"That's true, Mr. Ryder. Mr. Carson's damn good at it."

"Thanks, Chief. Artists like to be appreciated."

Romeo Corpen

Almost two dozen officers and enlisted men stood on the hangar deck at the open, fifty–foot door of Elevator 1, watching three dolphins leap and dive precisely halfway between the old Midway–class aircraft carrier USS Coral Sea (CVA–43), and the even older fleet oiler USS Passumpsic (AO–107), off to starboard. The Elevator 1 door provided a safe place to stand and get a good view of the dolphins. The sailors on the bridges and in the engine rooms of the two ships worked with intense concentration and quick reflexes to set, then maintain, the ordered constant speed and direction, a synchronous course called the *Romeo Corpen*. It was an unusually pleasant, breezy November Saturday morning on Yankee Station, the carrier staging area in the Tonkin Gulf, at 17 degrees 30 minutes north, 108 degrees 30 minutes east. The course was 195 degrees, the speed precisely 14 knots. The Officers of the Deck of the two ships had to maintain an exact spacing of 180 feet in order to keep the proper tension on the latticework of lines, spanwires, and hoses linking their vessels.

Underway replenishment operations— UNREPS—require skilled seamanship and intense concentration. This is especially true when a carrier takes on fuel, ordnance, and supplies. The carrier's size and massive flight deck overhang, make close–order maneuvering difficult. Because of their size and shape, carriers are slow to respond to—or "answer"—orders to change course and speed. Coming alongside an oiler, receiving the lines and hoses, then maintaining constant course, speed, and spacing demands as much concentration and skill as are expended during flight operations. Perhaps UNREPS demand even greater skill. Collisions between two ships are unlikely during flight ops. When refueling, they are a constant threat.

The dolphins appeared unconcerned with the rigors of course and speed. They maintained a perfect 14 knots, swimming in a straight line, 90 feet from each ship. Their navigation seemed effortless, maybe even mocking. To humans, dolphins always appear to be smiling. They don't smile of course. But that day they induced smiles from many of the men standing at Elevator 1 and from those manning the fueling stations.

During Tonkin Gulf UNREPS, two officers and about six or seven enlisted men stood on each fueling platform, spaces of roughly 10 x 15 feet, under the flight deck overhang, crowded with receiving pipes, winches, hoses, and block and tackle.

A junior officer—an Ensign or Lieutenant Junior Grade (LTJG)—from the Engineering Department and two enlisted Boilermen were there to see to the receiving of fuels. The Coral Sea required massive amounts of NSFO (Navy Special Fuel Oil) to run its antiquated, World War II, 600–pound steam propulsion system, while its airplanes ran on kerosene–based JP–5 (Jet Propulsion–5). The Deck Department assigned an Ensign or LTJG as "Safety Officer" on each platform. He and four enlisted men from the Deck Division attended to the winches, tensioners, and rigging.

The key man on the platform, however, was usually a second– or third–class Bosun's Mate, also from the Deck Department. He was the "rig captain," responsible for keeping the proper tension on the wires and lines supporting and controlling the fueling hoses.

The "rig captain" wore a yellow hardhat. The Safety Officer's was white, with a green cross, the winch operator's brown. Engineers wore gray hardhats. All wore bright orange life preservers. The dolphins required no safety equipment.

The enlisted men did all the work on the fueling platform. The two junior officers mainly tried to stay out of their way. Their job was to stand there for four or five hours, with no trips to the head and no smoke breaks. They would come into play only if something went seriously wrong. One of the Navy's oldest clichés is, "Somebody's got to hang." If a man fell overboard or a coupling gave way and thousands of gallons of NSFO were spilled, someone with a little rank had to be deemed responsible. He, or they, would face a court of inquiry, and perhaps a court–martial.

The two officers stood toward the back of the platform (against the ship's hull) and tried to remember to flex their knees frequently. They did their best not to think about it as their nicotine fits grew in intensity. But even for them, this UNREP was better than usual. They, too, could see the three dolphins.

Unlike the sailors on the fueling platforms, the men looking out from Elevator 1 did not need to be there. Some should have been at work; others could have been in their racks, resting up for their next watch on the bridge, in an engine room, in the galley, or in dozens of other work spaces. But they stood there, watching. A couple brought out Super–Eight movie cameras. Several ran for the expensive Japanese single–lens–reflex cameras that most Seventh Fleet sailors seemed to believe they were required to bring home. They shot whole rolls of Kodachrome slide film, trying over and over to catch the dolphins at the tops of their leaps.

Many "short–timers"—both enlisted men and officers—had not only become jaded about the Vietnam War and the Navy, but prided themselves in having done so. But for a few hours, in the shallowest corner of the South China Sea, they couldn't feel jaded. The dolphins' beauty and elegance overcame the sailors' affected indifference.

The dolphins didn't seem to tire. Well into their second hour of synchronized swimming with two U.S. Navy ships, they continued to leap, sometimes one after the other, sometimes simultaneously. "How do they *do* that?" the sailors occasionally asked each other. Frequently, men simply said in awed, subdued voices, "fucking beautiful."

While the *Romeo Corpen* held, nothing broke the mood. The ship–bound mammals respected and admired the unfettered mammals in the water. Sailors had once considered the company of dolphins good luck. But by 1969, superstition was no longer what it had been, at least in the Western Pacific. Now the dolphins were an elegant and entertaining—but transient—diversion from the normal mix of boredom and nervous tension endemic on combatant ships. Even the junior officers on the fueling platforms had forgotten the remote possibility of courts–martial.

At the end of Yankee Station UNREPS, the captains of the ships frequently agreed to conduct emergency breakaway drills. Ships linked together by numerous lines and hoses, locked into a *Romeo Corpen*, would be sitting ducks for enemy ships and airplanes, Therefore, the Navy has always considered it critical that crews to be trained to rapidly break all connections. Emergency breakaway drills do not allow the omission of any of the usual steps in securing supply operations; crews are expected to perform all prescribed steps, but more quickly. Either way, however, it is not a fast process. To speed it up significantly would almost certainly result in fatal accidents. In the Tonkin Gulf, emergency breakaway drills always reminded the crews that they should be grateful the North Vietnamese had neither submarines nor an air force. The drills had been useful in World War II. On Yankee Station in the 1960s, they were irrelevant.

The captains of the Coral Sea and the Passumpsic used the telephone line that is always passed over during UNREPS to set a precise time to commence their emergency breakaway drill. But the dolphins unilaterally broke off the

Romeo Corpen two minutes before the call for the drill sounded from the 1–MC loudspeaker systems of both ships. The watchers at Elevator 1 drifted away. The platform crews secured their operations quickly and carefully.

Within ten minutes after securing from the emergency breakaway drill, the Passumpsic had set a course for Subic Bay, Philippines, to take on another load of NSFO and JP–5. It would return to Yankee Station in three days. The Coral Sea's crew prepared for air ops; the first launches would commence in two hours. Where the dolphins were, nobody knew. Breaking off the *Romeo Corpen* had been easy for them. The sailors liked to think the dolphins were still smiling. But they knew better.

Late Casualties

"Never volunteer!"

"Something you learned in the navy, Chuck?" Cindy put down the stack of name tags.

"The navy reinforced it. But I've never mastered the lesson."

Cindy and Chuck were checking in a sporadic stream of hopefuls, wannabes, hacks, flakes, and some genuinely talented writers, for a weekend conference sponsored by the Capital City Mystery Club. Instead of the usual two–hour session in a public library meeting room, the Mystery Club had scheduled conference facilities at the Sheraton for the entire weekend. Cindy, the current president, had lined up two renowned authors. Carl Sanders, a retired Seattle detective, wrote popular police procedural novels. Wanda Truesdale's fourth novel was slowly descending from sixth place on the *New York Times* bestseller fiction list. Several critics said they expected her to surpass Patricia Cornwell in the medical mystery sub–genre. Pre–registrations were strong, but a week before the conference, Wanda Truesdale sent regrets, giving health reasons.

"Thanks again for persuading Lyle Smartt to step in on such short notice," Cindy said. "He complements the program, right down to the medical theme."

Lyle Smartt, a surgeon on the staff of the Veterans Administration hospital in Columbia, had served in the navy during the Vietnam War. Afterwards, he wrote two mystery novels. He based *Starboard Light* on his service on the aircraft carrier Mariana Straits; *Hospital Corners* drew on his time at Oak Knoll, a Naval Hospital in Oakland. He wrote his last book, *Murder in California*—a true crime story based on a double murder near California, Missouri—two decades after leaving the navy. Because he had seen numerous incision wounds—some in the aftermath of knife fights—during his naval service, the local medical examiner asked him to consult on that case.

His novels enjoyed moderate success. Indeed, thirty years later, a paperback edition of *Starboard Light* was still in print. But *Hospital Corners* was long out of print, and few copies of *Murder in California* had sold outside Missouri. Thereafter, Smartt apparently lost interest in writing. He devoted his time to his practice, which grew in inverse proportion to government cuts in VA funding. However, he still liked to attend mystery conferences.

Chuck had met Smartt at a mystery conference in Kansas City many years earlier. He found the doctor's books about the navy intriguing, especially since he, too, had spent almost two years on the Mariana Straits. He and Smartt figured out that they were on board at the same time for about two months, but neither could remember the other. This was not unusual on a ship carrying 4,200 men. They had stayed in touch since the Kansas City conference.

"He sure is generous with his time," Cindy said. ""He won't take a fee. He even waved off reimbursement for his expenses, and that's with gas at $2.98!"

At the cocktail party, Carl Sanders, the police procedural writer, received most of the attention. Most of the conferees tried to meet him, even if they were not particularly interested in his genre. Dr. Smartt drew little attention. Chuck tried to ensure that he was not totally ignored.

"Thanks again for filling in, Lyle. There's really a lot of interest in medical detective stories right now. Every writer seems to want to introduce a new Kay Scarpetta."

"Wanda Truesdale is going to be one of the best," Smartt said. "I would have been here to hear her anyhow."

A longtime club member walked up to Smartt and Chuck. Eddie Hebert and Chuck were old friends. Like Chuck and Lyle Smartt, Eddie had served in the Seventh Fleet. After reading *Starboard Light*, Eddie gathered his nerve, joined the Mystery Club, and started writing stories. He had recently sold his first to a webzine. "Hi, Chuck. Dr. Smartt, I'm Eddie Hebert. I'm happy to meet you. You're the reason I'm trying to learn to write. I've read all three of your books and wish there were more."

"Thanks. I'm glad you liked them."

"I especially like *Starboard Light*. "As far as I know, it is the only good novel about the Seventh Fleet during the war." To Eddie, Dr. Smartt, and Chuck, "the war" would always mean Vietnam.

"My brother was on a carrier. You really caught the feel for what the war was like for him. I was on two Seventh Fleet oilers, taking fuel out to the carriers and destroyers."

"That's a lot of unreps," Smartt said, using the slang word for "underway replenishment." Eddie reached into a tote bag from a public radio fund drive, pulled out a book, and held it out to Smartt. It was clothbound, with a smudged and torn dust cover.

"Would you mind autographing *Starboard Light* for me, Doc? I've read it any number of times."

Smartt pulled out a pen. "I'll bet you're one of few who has."

"He really has, Lyle. He must have lost his library card," said Chuck.

With a flourish, Dr. Smartt inscribed the title page, "To Eddie, a fellow Seventh Fleet sailor and writer, as well as a glutton for punishment!" He added his signature and handed it back. "Typical doctor's handwriting, I'm afraid."

"Thanks, Doc, I'm going to shove off and let some of your other fans meet you. I'll look forward to hearing your talk in the morning."

As Eddie left, a slim woman nursing a Miller Lite approached. Chuck had never seen her before. She reached out to shake hands.

"Good evening Doctor. I'm Dottie Fowlkes, from Vichy, the one here in Missouri."

"Hello sir," she said to Chuck. "Thank you for bringing Dr. Smartt in. He's the one who drew me to this conference."

"Another fan, Lyle," Chuck said.

"Yes. It's great to see both my readers on the same evening."

"Another beer, Lyle?"

"Much appreciated, Chuck. Thanks." He turned toward the woman. "Dottie Fowlkes, that sounds familiar. . . ."

"Fowlkes is my married name. My maiden name is Jenrette."

"Oh. That's a name I'm afraid I'm never going to forget. Paul and Lisa . . . ?"

"My brother and sister," Fowlkes replied.

Paul and Lisa Jenrette were the teenaged stabbing victims whose deaths he had written about in *Death in California*. The police stopped a biker with a long criminal record who had camped on the Jenrette's farm for a few days. They found a bloody knife in his saddlebag. DNA analysis was not available then, but the type matched Paul Jenrette's. Smartt assured the medical examiner that the blade was consistent with the wounds to both victims. The biker yelled that he had never seen the knife. During transport to the courthouse for arraignment, the biker escaped, helped by several fellow gang members, as well as the incompetence of the Sheriff's Office. The biker and his gang stayed on the run for almost two weeks, until the Kansas Highway Patrol caught up with them, killing the accused biker and one of his gang. "You know, I've never been convinced that we learned the whole story," Smartt said.

"I agree with you, Doctor," she said. "It has been nice meeting you, but I'm afraid I had better excuse myself before I start crying. I'll see you at your session in the morning."

Chuck returned, handed Smartt a John Adams, and said, "She didn't look too good."

"Sad memories."

Dr. Smartt had the eight o'clock slot on Saturday morning, traditionally a poor placement in weekend conferences. It is often noon by the time everyone arrives, and some of the people who arrived the night before decide to sleep in. Because attendance is inevitably lower in Saturday morning sessions, they provide the poorest opportunity to shill books.

Since leaving the navy, Chuck rarely got up early on Saturday mornings. But he did what he had to do. About forty people of various ages, ethnicities, and writing abilities had already gathered in the Sheraton's Garden Room by the time he arrived. Lyle Smartt was ready, his notes on the podium, copies of his books on a table at the back of the room. Chuck introduced the doctor, thanked him for filling in, and reminded the conferees that Dr. Smartt would autograph copies of his books at the end of the session.

Just as Smartt started talking, a man of about sixty, bald, overweight, and without a conference name tag, jumped to his feet and began to yell, "This man is a liar! He destroys his colleagues' good names and their lives!" Red–faced and sweating, the fat man screamed obscenities and invective, accusing Smartt of all manner of evil. "He put my wife in her grave!"

Smartt said nothing. He gripped the top of the podium with both hands; his jaw tightened and his complexion paled, but otherwise he did not respond. Chuck tried to stop the man. Eddie

Hebert got up to help. Each grabbed one of the man's arms and they hustled him out of the room. The man kept yelling, but allowed himself to be steered out. Once Chuck, Eddie, and the fat man cleared the room, Smartt released the podium and said, "I'm sorry this happened here. This gentleman has suffered a series of misfortunes for which he believes I'm responsible. His quarrels are entirely with me; they have nothing to do with you, this conference, or mystery writing, which is what we are here to talk about."

Smartt began his presentation as Chuck and Eddie rejoined the group. "When we write about times and events our readers have lived through, they—and we—sometimes have trouble letting go of the past. The attachment can be highly emotional. This is not often a problem when authors set books in the old west or in Elizabethan England. If writing fiction about the recent past is indeed riskier, why do some of us do it? Why not write either about pasts further removed or simply about the present? I would suggest that for most of us who set mysteries—or other fiction for that matter—in the recent past, it is primarily because we have lived in interesting and often baffling times. The Gulf Wars, the war in Iraq, Nine–Eleven, the digitalization of global society, and Bill and Monica, for example, are crucial and fascinating. All of them provide rich ground for novels, including mysteries.

"For many people of my rapidly aging generation, the Vietnam War is an enduring presence. As William Faulkner said of the South, 'The past is not dead. In fact, it's not even past.' The same is true of the United States in Vietnam. It is true for the combat soldiers and pacifists, draft evaders and marines, and all the families and friends who lived with the dread of harm to their loved ones and with the fury of politics on the home front. And as far as that misbegotten war goes, I believe the best fiction has not yet been written. Even for people of my age, it has been hard to write with absolute candor. As graphic as the fictional murders were in my two books set during the war, I could not really describe the truth, which to me, seemed worse. I could not trivialize the sacrifice—and the nobility—of some of my shipmates, or of the wounded who came back through Oak Knoll Hospital. I want to give you an example of an incident I still have not been able to write about. I've only recently been able to talk about it.

"Like any crowded workplace, a ship has its share of rivalries and feuds, both petty and grand. But at the same time, the devotion to shipmates is unqualified. Sailors can be jerks—actually the word in common use was "assholes"—one moment, heroes the next.

172

"While I based *Starboard Light* on my experiences on the Mariana Straits, by then I had already served a couple of months on the Coral Sea, another Midway–class aircraft carrier. One night on the Coral Sea, a Sidewinder—a heat-seeking missile—somehow got loose on the forward ordinance assembly area, adjacent to the mess decks and the first–class lounge, a separate area where ranking petty officers could drink coffee, play cards, read, and so forth. When the Sidewinder took off, it penetrated the bulkhead of the First–Class Lounge and lodged there. It didn't fully fire, thank God, or it would have killed any number of men.

"The collision of the missile and the bulkhead threw off some shrapnel. A couple of pieces hit a first class boatswain's mate, or "bosun," in the chest, breaking several ribs, collapsing his lungs, and causing massive internal injuries, with copious bleeding. Another piece of shrapnel almost severed the right forearm of a first class machinist's mate, causing heavy venous bleeding. Another piece hit him near the right eye, filling it with blood. The machinist somehow—and I still can't understand how—used his left hand and teeth to tie his ripped and bloody right sleeve into a tourniquet. With his left hand and arm, he picked up the bosun and headed for sick bay. Somebody phoned the bridge and the OOD immediately sounded general quarters, so I reached the hatch and ladder leading down to Sick Bay at about the same time as the machinist's mate, who was carrying the bosun.

"The hospital corpsmen, the other two doctors, and I managed to get the machinist's mate and the bosun onto examination tables. I was the only surgeon. I had to make one of those awful wartime choices. The bosun had virtually no chance, while the machinist had lost an awful lot of blood, had had an eye put out, and was close to death. I hoped by amputating the arm, tying off the veins, and pouring in plasma, we could possibly—*possibly*, not *probably*—save him. So I grabbed one of the other doctors and told him to assist me. I told the third doctor to do what he could for the bosun. But I knew that other than giving him as much morphine as possible, there was nothing to do. And right then, somebody yelled, 'No!' Who do you think that might have been?"

"One of the other doctors?"

"A corpsman?"

"Nope," Smartt said. "The machinist. He said he could hold on; we had to do our best for the other guy. He was wrong, of course. We did what we had to do. We decided to try to save his life, and the bosun died. But there's more. I learned shortly afterwards that the bosun and the machinist had been feuding for months. During the last yard period in San Francisco, the machinist's girlfriend had eloped to Reno with the bosun. And yet, the machinist had put his life on the line, trying to save his shipmate by getting him to safety, then insisting that the man get immediate treatment, when he, himself, was bleeding to death. I've never seen anything like it. And as noble as it was, I hope never to see such a thing again."

Smartt paused, then took a drink of water. "That's what I meant about simultaneous nobility and tragedy. I hope to be able to write about the carrier navy again. If I can find a respectful enough way to use that story, I will. But when I was writing *Starboard Light*, it just overcame me. I couldn't handle it. How can you use such a story in a mystery novel without sounding mawkish, and exploitative? Only by separating it from oneself in time, I would argue. It can take a while to develop the necessary perspective and the humanity. Critics of mystery writing would say such a story is improbable, if not preposterous. I would agree that it is improbable. But it happened."

Smartt maintained a quiet, deliberate manner. Without reaching for dramatic effect, he had produced it. The audience, including the inevitable latecomers, was subdued. Most were looking down. Eddie abruptly stood up and left. Dottie Fowlkes soon followed.

Smartt took questions about whether war settings provided good settings for mysteries, and whether mysteries could actually build on the brutality and moral ambiguity of war. Then he thanked the audience and took a seat at the table in the back of the room. He sold and signed about a dozen books, mainly *Starboard Light*.

As the last purchaser left, Chuck said, "Lyle, what was that old guy's outburst at the beginning about? "

"I guess I owe you and Cindy an explanation. His name is Stanley Hobbes. He used to be a general practitioner in Columbia. He also did minor surgeries, like gall bladders and appendectomies. Needless to say he wasn't board certified in surgery. He caused any number of patients unnecessary pain and suffering, and almost certainly killed some of them. The Boone County Medical Association decided that it just had no choice but to initiate the process of pulling his medical license. Unfortunately, I was the chairman of the association at the time. He lost his license, his practice, and his place in the community.

"Not surprisingly, he centered his anger on me. When his wife had a stroke and died, he blamed that on me. Now he scrapes along on investment income, bitter but not quite defeated.

He petitions for reinstatement, but that isn't going to happen. He has taken to showing up once or twice a year at public events I'm attending. He tries to have his say while everybody walks away, or he is taken out, like you did today. He is a suffering, but harmless, soul. I' sorry he did this at your conference."

"It wasn't your fault, Lyle. It's a shame that you have to endure something like that. Thank you again for helping us out of a real hole. Wouldn't you like to stick around for the rest of the conference? You could really help the authors' round table at lunch tomorrow."

"Sorry, Chuck. I'm on call back in Columbia, starting this evening. Besides, it is probably best if all the participants on your panel are people who are writing *now*."

Chuck walked nest door to the Terrace Room to make sure that it was set up for the next presentation. The speakers and audience were already beginning to gather. He heard Cindy yelling, "Chuck! Chuck!" He turned and she almost ran into him.

Somebody tried to kill Dr. Smartt!"

Chuck grabbed her on the shoulders. "Is he okay? Where is he?"

"At the side door! Chuck!"

He pulled his cell phone out of its belt clip and dialed 911. A dispatcher told him that someone had already reported the attack on another line, so help was on the way. He ran out the side door of the hotel nearest the Garden Room. Just outside the door, Smart lay on his side with his hands pressed to his abdomen. Blood covered the flagstones and decorative rocks on the path between the door and the parking lot. A row of Scotch Pines partially screened the area. The ambulance charged into the lot in less than four minutes; a patrol car followed a minute later. The EMT's quickly loaded Smartt into the ambulance and rushed away. The police taped off the immediate area, finishing just as two detectives arrived. When they asked who was in charge of the event, Chuck said, "Uh, Cindy Finch, our president, I guess."

The detectives asked Chuck and Cindy to do their best to herd the conference registrants back into the rooms they had been in at the time of—or just before—the 911 call, and to give them a roster. Chuck did his best to get all of those who had attended Smartt's session back into the Garden Room. He and Cindy asked the late arrivals and those who skipped the first session, to take a seat in the lobby, where Cindy could keep an eye on them.

Sergeant Jeffries, the older of the two detectives, went into the Garden Room with Chuck. He asked if everyone who had been there for Smartt's talk was in the room now. Chuck went over the registration list, looking at all the names that had been checked off, meaning that they had at least come in the room.

"I don't see Dottie Fowlkes," Chuck said. "Has anyone seen her in the last few minutes?"

"What about the lunatic?" Eddie Hebert asked.

"Oh, yeah," Chuck said. "He wouldn't have been on the list. Smartt said his name was Stanley something. Hobbes." He told Sergeant Jeffries what Smartt had told the conferees about the about the unfortunate doctor.

One of the patrolmen came into the room and motioned Sergeant Jeffries to a corner. The two men whispered briefly and the patrolman handed the detective a plastic bag containing a solid object. Jeffries said, "The emergency room doctor just pronounced Dr. Smartt DOA. Then he held up the bag and asked, "Did anybody see a knife like this today? Maybe somebody was picking his nails with it, or opening a pack of junk food?"

A sudden hollowness in his chest and shakiness in his legs almost forced Chuck to sit down. The knife had been made by Buck, a family–held company, in Post Falls, Idaho. It was an extremely popular folding hunter, with smooth wooden handles, brass bolsters, liners, and rivets, and a three–and–three–quarter-inch blade. This one was obviously an older model, with dull brass and a beat up grip. Chuck had the same model in his glove compartment, or he hoped he still did.

Sergeant Jeffries allowed Chuck to take a closer look. A trace of blood had leaked out of the handle. Chuck saw could now tell this was not his knife. The handles were heavily worn, with a large gouge on the right side. Much relieved, Chuck tried not to change his expression as he handed the bagged knife back.

Sergeant Jeffries said the knife had been found closed, under one of the cars in the most crowded part of the parking lot. "Most likely, the guy who used it wiped it off, but had no time to hide it, so he threw it under a car, hoping nobody would notice it for a while."

"Please stay here," the sergeant said as he opened the door to leave. "Some officers will come to take your statements."

"I guess that's the end of the conference," said Bethany Little, the only teenaged member of the Mystery Club.

An elderly man asked, "Are we going to get some money back?" Chuck knew that Sid Kramer lived on little more than social security. The Mystery Club was one of his few indulgences.

Eddie changed the subject. "For such a nice man, Doc Smartt sure had some enemies."

"Do you mean Dr. Hobbes?" Chuck asked.

"He's one of them."

"I'll bet it was him," said Bethany Little. "He just got too wrought up this time."

"You're probably right," Eddie said.

Chuck sat down at the table nearest the podium. "Let's leave that for the police."

"Just what the hell was Dottie Fowlkes doing here?" Sid Kramer asked.

"Chuck sat up a little. "What do you mean, Sid?" Wasn't she here for a mystery writers conference, like the rest of us?"

"Then where is she?"

"I don't know, Sid. Where?"

Sid ignored the question. "I've heard that Dr. Smartt was never really satisfied with that investigation he wrote about in *Death in California*. Blaming everything on that motorcycle freak didn't really satisfy him. I do know that he went back to California a month or two ago to talk with the chief of police.

"What would that have to do with Dottie Fowlkes?" Chuck was incredulous.

Sid was loaded for bear. "She was a teenager when her brother and sister got killed. Some folks say she had herself a reputation back then, that she was the kind of girl who would hang out with a motorcycle gang."

"Now wait a minute, Mr. Kramer!" Bethany was livid. "Are you saying that because Ms. Fowlkes

181

was a teenager, maybe a little wild, she must have had something to do with her brother's and sister's murders?"

Sid couldn't quit. "I'm not saying anything except where there's smoke there's generally fire. And it looks like Dr. Smartt was starting to stir up things again. That might worry some folks who'd rather leave things alone."

Bethany clinched her fists. "Mr. Kramer, I'd be quiet if I were you. When the police track down Dr. Hobbes and prove he killed Dr. Smartt, Ms. Fowlkes will probably sue you for slander."

The others in the room started taking sides, shouting either at—or in support of—Sid or Bethany. The clamor built. Chuck decided it was time to put an end to it. He walked to the back of the room where Eddie had been sitting alone, head in his hands, ignoring the argument. Chuck spoke quietly.

"Eddie, let's not do this here. Let's go out in the hall. You can take my phone and call Bill Powell." Eddie's head snapped up.

"What the hell are you talking about?"

"Eddie, I know Bill's not a criminal lawyer, but he knows them all and he'll get you a good one."

"What are you saying, Chuck? Are you nuts?"

"Eddie. I'm sorry. I could tell you were as surprised as I was when Lyle Smartt said he had been on the Coral Sea at the time of that

Sidewinder accident. I knew that was the way your brother Roy died. As well as I knew Lyle, I didn't know he had ever been on the Coral Sea."

Eddie looked down silently; his grief profound.

"Eddie, take my phone."

"Why would a surgeon work on a man who would probably have survived anyway, instead of a man that needed all his skills?" Eddie yelled, almost silencing the Hobbes vs. Fowlkes argument in the front of the room.

"That's not the way he saw it, Eddie."

Eddie said, "I might as well tell you all what happened." Chuck begged him again to call Bill Powell and to keep his mouth shut. The room was silent, but a good third of the people had opened their notebooks.

"My brother Roy and I both joined the navy and ended up in the Seventh Fleet, in the Western Pacific, but not on the same ship. He was the bosun's mate that Dr. Smartt told us about last night. The one he decided not to treat. Until this morning, I didn't know Dr. Smartt had ever been on the Coral Sea. Then he told us that he decided to just let Roy die! The choice was all his! I just couldn't take it."

"Eddie, shut the hell up!"

"When he was on his way out of the building, I tried to talk to him," Eddie said. "I *had* to ask him why he hadn't even tried to save Roy.

Roy was all I had, my only family. I asked him why he couldn't at least *try*! He just shook his head and kept walking. I tried to make him stop and just *talk* to me. He pushed my arm away and told me to leave him alone. I just couldn't listen any more. I lost it. I took out my pocketknife, and just poked at him."

"I asked him how it felt. He started to back off; I tried to keep the knife on him. I must have hit an artery. He fell. I figured he had no chance. I closed the knife, wiped it on a pine branch, closed it, and skidded it under the cars in the crowded part of the parking lot. Then I came back in." Eddie sighed, sat down, and put his head in his hands.

He looked at Chuck. "It was the knife, wasn't it. You didn't really know before, did you?"

"Yeah, Eddie," Chuck said, "it was the knife."

Then, Chuck, speaking to everyone in the room, explained that this Buck knife had been one of the most popular tools in the fleet. "Bosuns Mates and anyone else who worked around lines, and especially on unreps, liked them. If someone out on one of those little platforms got caught in a line, or if the gears on a winch grabbed the laces on your life preserver, a fast, sharp knife might save your life. A lot of former sailors still have their old Bucks. I do. When I was on an unrep station, just like Eddie's brother, Roy, I wanted the best blade."

Chuck turned to Eddie. "Was that Roy's knife?"

"Yeah, he had it on him when the Sidewinder went off. I've carried it ever since. Every time I cut a rope or opened a big bag of dog food with it, I thought of Roy. "

"Let's go outside and call Bill Powell. You gotta get a lawyer," Chuck said. Eddie, slumped and shakey, followed obediently.

Chuck and Cindy declared the conference over. They would decide tomorrow what to do about fees, refunds, and the like. After seeing off all the people who had attended, they went into the Sheraton's bar. Cindy ordered a scotch and soda.

"Wild Turkey, a double, straight up," Chuck told the bartender.

"It's 2006 and we have two more victims of Vietnam," Cindy said. Is that war *never* going to end?"

Chuck took a long sip of the 100–proof whiskey. "Not until the last damned one of us is dead."

Bad Day at Captain's Mast

On a perfect spring morning with flat seas and clear blue skies, Captain Eli P. Cooke made a terrible mistake. He decided it was a good day for Captain's Mast. And he decided to make an example out of one member of the crew.

On 25 April 1969, the aging aircraft carrier Mariana Straits (CVA–44) completed five months of its scheduled seven–month WESTPAC deployment. After a five–day in–port period at Subic Bay, Philippines, it was steaming at a steady twenty–five knots back to the Yankee Station staging area in the Tonkin Gulf. In about forty hours, the Mariana Straits and its air wing of A–6 and A–7 intruders and F–4 Phantoms would recommence air operations, consisting of bombing runs over North Vietnam and Laos.

As usual after a port call, a couple of dozen crewmen had been placed on report for violations of various naval regulations. The most frequent were barroom fights, being picked up by the Shore Patrol entering or leaving areas posted as Out–of–Bounds, and Unauthorized Absence (UA). Virtually all of the offenses involved alcohol and women—bar girls working in the saloons along Raymon Magsaysay Drive, in the city of Olongapo, which bordered the U.S. Naval Base at Subic Bay. Such offenses were disposed of at Captain's Mast. Captain's Mast is the naval term for Nonjudicial Punishment, or NJP. Under Article 15 of the *Uniform Code of Military Justice*, the commanding officer of a ship is authorized to hand down penalties in the case of offenses that do not justify courts–martial.

Captain Eli P. Cooke knew he could not afford major mistakes on his ship. So did every officer and enlisted man serving in the crew and in the air wing on board the Mariana Straits. During the late 1960s, relatively few Navy pilots who reached the rank of captain were assigned command of aircraft carriers. Those few awarded command stood a decent chance of being selected for a rear admiral's star, which could lead to more stars. However, a perceived failure meant the Captain would be encouraged to consider early retirement. Whether a carrier captain made admiral, or was eased out of the Navy, depended upon an appraisal of his performance—and those of his ship, air wing, and crew.

Captain Cooke wanted to be an admiral. He wanted it badly. Thus, he knew that not only did the air wing need to turn in a better–than–usual performance, he had to see that no one on his ship made a major mistake. If an Officer of the Deck made an erroneous turn resulting in a collision or near collision, or slammed into a pier or bridge piling, the Commanding Officer would be held responsible. The Navy's standard of performance for a carrier captain was high and harsh. A catastrophic accident, such as the disastrous fires on the Forrestal and the Oriskany would lead to the C.O. being relieved of command, and—at the very least—hustled out of the service. Even a ship's reputation for having an unusually unruly crew might cost the Captain. In short, no matter what happened, the lines of accountability were clear. They all led to the C.O.

Like most carrier C.O.s, Cooke hated Captain's Mast. This morning he wanted to make short work of the two dozen cases before him. Rather than going below to the Legal Office, he decided to hold Mast on the starboard wing of the bridge. When Legal Office Yeoman Second Class Web Baird came up to the bridge with an armful of manila folders, Cooke asked if they were the usual offenses. "Pretty much, Sir," Baird said, "brawls and UAs."

"I've never understood why so many men are willing to go on report for unauthorized absences," the C.O. said.

Baird knew this was not an invitation to conversation. "No telling, Sir." Except when he glanced over the folders, Cooke never took his eyes off the horizon. His Marine orderly, Corporal Gritman, placed a podium on the bridge wing, then took all but one of the folders from the C.O., handed them back to Baird, and said, "We are ready to proceed, Sir."

Bringing the miscreants and their division officers before the podium in proper order was Corporal Gritman's job. "Call the first case," Captain Cooke said. The initial dozen cases were routine, even boring—five brawls and seven UAs. Even so, the C.O. made a point of looking away from the horizon and making eye contact with each offender, and his division officer. He began with a tendency towards leniency. For the brawlers, Captain Cooke assigned twenty hours each of Extra Military Instruction (EMI), the Navy's euphemism for physically taxing and mind–numbingly boring work details, to be performed when the offender was not on watch. The UAs demanded greater discretion. Five of the absences were for less than two hours. Cooke considered light EMI assignments just and appropriate. In one case, a sailor was five hours late getting back to the ship. The C.O. assigned him considerably more hours of EMI.

Yeoman Baird handed the Captain the thirteenth report file of the morning. Corporal Gritman called in Fireman James Jeffries and B Division Officer Lieutenant Junior Grade George Paige. They stood at attention, facing the Captain. "Mr. Paige, I believe this is the third man from your division I've seen already this morning. And if memory serves me correctly, this is the third Captain's Mast in which B Division has led the way."

Paige maintained a poker face. "Yes, Sir."

"Is B Division trying for a record in bad behavior?"

"No, Sir," said LTJG Paige.

Captain Cooke then addressed Jeffries. "I see you were UA for three days."

The slight, pale, nineteen–year–old fireman answered, "Yes, Sir."

"And the Shore Patrol picked you up leaving a designated Out–of–Bounds area?"

"Yes, Sir."

The C.O. stared at the charge sheet. "So Jeffries, why did you go UA for three days, and why were you arrested for being Out–of–Bounds?"

Jeffries managed to squirm yet still stand at attention. "I just got engaged. I couldn't stand to leave Elaina, my fiancée."

"A bar girl?"

"Not any more, Sir. She used to work at the Straw Hat Club, but I told her she would have to quit that and she said 'okay'."

The Captain, LTJG Paige, Yeoman Baird, and even Corporal Gritman had heard this story before. The latter two rolled their eyes; Captain Cooke pretended not to notice. "Are you aware that naval regulations prohibit enlisted personnel from marrying foreign nationals without permission?"

"But isn't permission always given, Sir?" Jeffries's voice took on an edge of anxiety.

"It is by no means assured, Jeffries. I wouldn't count on it," the Captain said. He shifted his eye contact to LTJG Paige. "What kind of sailor is Jeffries, Mr. Paige?"

Paige of course could not simply say that Jeffries was a total and perpetual screw–up. Nor was he expected to. "I would call Jeffries a good, average fireman, Sir."

A total screw–up then, the C.O. said to himself. He knew the code.

According to the procedures specified for NJP, Captain Cooke was required to either assign a punishment—or choose not to—immediately. It was Captain Bligh or Mr. Roberts, on the spot. *Bligh!* The C.O. had been too lenient with too many offenders up to this point, but three days UA—

combined with blatant stupidity—called for a stern response. That had been his assessment when he read the charge sheet on Jeffries earlier that morning. Nothing he heard at Mast had changed it. "Fireman Jeffries, you will perform sixty hours of EMI. You will be restricted to the ship for the duration of this deployment. And I will recommend against granting you permission to marry a Filipina."

Jeffries and the others present realized immediately that it was unlikely that he would ever see his "fiancé" again. Everyone except Jeffries knew from experience that he would take the loss a good deal more seriously than would the bar girl.

The sailor's knees buckled and his face turned even pastier. "Please, Sir, don't do this. I'll never go UA again." But he offered no resistance when Corporal Gritman hustled him off the bridge. The entire ship knew about the NJP before Jeffries even reached Boiler Room 8. Information does not travel—quickly or otherwise—on a ship. Rather, it suddenly envelopes the vessel like a squall.

Jeffries complained vehemently to anyone who would listen. He was going to fight the Captain's punishment, he said. He took the ancient and sardonic naval suggestion that he "tell it to the chaplain." The protestant chaplain, familiar with and weary of nineteen–year–olds' infatuations with Asian bar girls, tried to console Jeffries without encouraging him.

Jeffries went to the ship's legal officer. "Sir, can the C.O. get away with this?"

The legal officer said, "Yes. He is acting well within the rights of a ship's commanding officer."

When Jeffries was finally convinced that no one would help him, he began to indulge in revenge fantasies. Like every man on board, he was aware that Captain Cooke was effectively on probation with the Seventh Fleet and Pentagon brass, and that his record on this deployment of the Mariana Straits was critical to him. Jeffries wondered what he could do to foul up the Captain's record, and still keep himself out of the Navy's prison at Portsmouth, New Hampshire. Fantasies of overcoming the helmsman and turning the ship onto a collision course with another vessel, or running it aground, were briefly enjoyable.

But Jeffries knew there was no realistic chance of even getting onto the bridge. He considered sabotaging Boiler Room 8. But the Midway Class carriers could run at flank speed on only eight of their twelve boilers. Indeed, they did so daily. He could think of no way to sabotage one of the four main engines or shafts.

Almost three weeks after the Captain's Mast, a pair of electrician's mates sat down across the table from Jeffries on the forward mess decks.

One of them had served on the Oriskany (CVA–34), an even older carrier than the Mariana Straits, during its major fire in October, 1966. "Yeah, that was bad shit," the older electrician said. "Forty–four men killed, more than thirty of them pilots sleeping in their racks." The younger electrician said, "I heard it was started by a parachute flare."

"Yeah," said the older man, "an airman got curious. He got into a flare locker up on the 01 deck. He didn't know shit about flares; he was just skylarking. He accidentally lit off one of the flares. Those mothers burn at 1800 degrees, so he couldn't hold onto it. The dumbass panicked and threw it back into the locker and it touched off all of the other flares."

"Forty–four men?" the second electrician said in a hushed tone.

"It took three hours to get the fire out. And the whole ship might have gone up. The red shirts had already started taking ordnance up to load the planes for the first launch when the fire started. Men started rolling bombs over the side. They pushed the aircraft on the flight deck and the hangar deck aft, as far away from the fire as they could. Some men got into oxygen breathing apparatuses and went into the pilots' berthing spaces and hauled out men overcome by smoke. A bunch of men got medals after that day. They deserved every damn one of them, and more. I don't get sentimental, but that was one time I felt damned proud to be a sailor."

Jeffries spoke up. "What did the airman do wrong? I mean, what is the right way to light off one flare and not set off all the others?"

The older electrician said, "The best way is to keep your damn hands off 'em."

After a thirty–five day line period, with bombing operations on all but three days, the Mariana Straits tied up in Sasebo, Japan, for a five–day port call. Jeffries was ready, even though he couldn't leave the ship. While determined to shitcan the Captain's naval career, he didn't want to kill or hurt anybody. After some scouting, he had located a flare locker in one of the air wing's ready rooms. An in–port fire, especially one well forward on the 01 deck, should have little chance of loss of life, or even catastrophic damage to the ship. All of the bombs would be stowed below decks, inside the magazines. The aircraft would be aft, mainly on the hangar deck. And if the fire took place in the evening, all the pilots would likely be off the ship, either enjoying Sasebo or pulling Shore Patrol watches.

At 2100, Jeffries went down to Boiler Room 8 to pick up a pair of bolt cutters he had hidden, along with a flashlight. He moved up the ladders to the 01 deck, then walked all the way forward.

The ready room with the flare locker was on the port side, away from the pier. He switched on the flashlight and used the bolt cutters to remove the padlock from the flare locker. In a crude extrapolation from the story of the Oriskany fire, he had guessed that half–a–dozen flares should be sufficient to create a spectacular fire that would do significant damage, but not kill anybody or touch off secondary explosions. He walked to the far port side of the ready room, bundled five flares with a rubber band, and removed their plastic caps. Then he walked into the passageway outside the ready room, putting some space between him and the flare locker. He placed the bundle on the deck and moved away from it. He removed the cap from the sixth flare and struck its tip against the built–in striker.

Jeffries figured that he could ignite the single flare, set it down about ten feet from the bundle, and then run far enough to escape the flash when single flare ignited the bundle. He figured wrong. The heat and brilliant flash of the single flare blinded him. Like the airman on the Oriskany, he panicked. He dropped the flare and ran blindly. He smashed his head into a stanchion just as the bundled flares went off.

The fire burned for most of an hour before the in–port damage control party could completely extinguish it. Jeffries was right. Loss of life was minimal, just one man. Captain Cooke had to send a letter to the parents of James Jeffries, explaining that their son had lost his life in a tragic shipboard accident. He was mourned by all his shipmates, the C.O. said.

On 24 April 1970, Eli P. Cooke played golf in La Jolla, as he had done at least three times a week since his retirement. George Paige taught five twelfth–grade social studies classes in Rice Lake, Wisconsin. In Austin, Texas, Web Baird yawned through another day of law school classes. And at Camp Lejeune, North Carolina, John Gritman received his staff sergeant's stripes.

On the other side of the International Date Line, where it was already 25 April, the Mariana Straits was tied up at Pier Three in Subic Bay. A mile away, in Olongapo, Quartermaster Third Class Ken Guthrie listened to a young Filipina named Elaina assure him that she would not only marry him, she would stop working as a bar girl at the Straw Hat Club on Ramon Magsaysay Drive.

Choose Your Hell

Sleep came hard to Lance. Personnel problems, always personnel problems. That was his job— dealing with whining employees, bitching employees, defiant employees who "knew their rights." And the union contract made it damn near impossible to fire anyone for anything. Only lovely fantasies of telling his boss to take his job and shove it finally calmed him enough to drift off.

A scratchy recording of a familiar trumpet tune blasted him awake and off his mattress. His head hit something less than two feet above. He had to roll—not rise—off the surface he had been sleeping on, a piece of canvas lashed tightly onto an aluminum frame. Another stretched canvas was lashed above his, and one below it. There were similar rigs on three sides of the room that was now filled with men milling around in their underwear, paying no attention to the brass music booming from speakers in the corners.

When the tune ended, a bass voice boomed, "Now reveille, reveille. All hands heave out and trice up. The smoking lamp is lighted throughout the ship." Again, none of the muttering, milling men paid any attention.

Where the hell am I? After another moment's concentration, Lance knew. *I'm in Hell.*

He found himself falling in with the other men, most of whom appeared younger than he. *And I'm younger than me, too.* Like them, he went to a locker at the head of the canvas rack where he had slept. He pulled out a shaving kit and walked into a six–sink, four toilet, three urinal bathroom. He found an open sink, brushed his teeth and shaved. He yawned and walked back to his rack. Like the others, he pulled out bell–bottomed dungarees, a chambray work shirt, and a pair of dull black shoes. He continued to do what he saw the other men do.

So we all dress the same way in Hell. And there are no women here. That's odd.

Strangely, he always seemed to know what to do next. He climbed up a ladder, turned into a hallway, and headed left. He found himself pushing a steel tray along a cafeteria line. One at a time, the men in front of him held their trays out to men wearing white and ladling out food.

"Powdered eggs and shit–on–a–shingle again," the man in front of Lance said. Lance held out his tray. *I don't think I'm going to like Hell.*

He took a seat on a bench attached to one of many long steel–and–formica tables, then reflected on Hell as he chewed on his lukewarm chipped beef on toast. *It's not really pleasant, but at least there's no physical pain. And best of all, it's not excessively hot. It can't be more than 80° F in here.*

Strangely, he could even converse knowledgeably with the other men at the table. The cost of beer and the bar girls in Olongapo dominated the conversation. *How is it that I know so much about sin in the Philippines?*

He finished breakfast, dumped out his tray into a garbage bin, then placed it on a rack. He headed up a long passageway. Without having to think, he knew where to go and what to do. He took ladders down three levels; he knew the levels were called "decks." He realized he was on an old Navy aircraft carrier called the Mariana Straits, and that his job was to supervise the next watch in boiler room 2 Alfa. He met a man whose uniform was khaki, not denim. The man— his Chief—said, "Go over to 2 Charlie and take the top watch there. We're going to secure and rebrick 2 Alfa."

"Aye, aye, Chief." Again, all of the jobs and jargon made sense to Lance, even though he had never heard them before. He entered boiler room 2 Charlie, assigned the other three men there to various tasks, then lit a Pall Mall. *I smoke?*

In an epiphany, he knew he was no longer Lance. He was Gary Wilson, a second–class boilerman, living and working on an aircraft carrier in the Tonkin Gulf in September of 1968. He had ceased to be a personnel officer for the regional headquarters of a national insurance company.

While shipboard life resembled the picture he had often carried of Hell, his fellow "devils" were not as bad as he thought they would be. And they were not nearly as hard to listen to as his fellow insurance company employees. Since arriving here, he had not had to talk with a single complaining employee who expected him to solve his or her problems. While boiler room 2 Charlie looked and almost felt like his picture of an inferno, for now it beat the yammering malcontents at the insurance company office. Maybe Hell really was other people, as some author Lance vaguely remembered from college had said. But while Lance had gone to college, Gary Wilson had not. So the name Camus did not come to him.

When he turned over the 2 Charlie boiler room top watch at 1400, BT2 Gary Wilson knew it was time for a shower and a fresh uniform. Someone had told him to report to the ship's Photo Center. One of the ship's photographers prepared to pictures. The Captain of the Mariana

Straits handed him a pen and said, "Put your John Hancock on this line, son."

Gary Wilson thought, *And why am I signing on for another four years of sweat and shit–on–a–shingle? All life must be Hell. Not everybody gets to choose where to serve it.* "Aye, aye, Sir."

The Red Shirt Record

Captain Miles Carter took pride in his ship's remarkable safety record. During its current deployment, the USS Mariana Straits (CVA–44) had suffered neither flight deck nor hangar deck accidents, no fires or explosions, and no major violations of safety regulations as it carried out its mission, conducting bombing runs over North Vietnam and Laos. Indeed, no accident had marred the Mariana Straits's record on its previous tour, under another commanding officer. Like all captains, Carter wanted his ship and its crew to excel, to be recognized. And he, personally, had a great deal on the line.

The few naval pilots selected to command aircraft carriers in the Vietnam War were given a single deployment to the war zone—the Tonkin Gulf—to compile a record that might lead to selection for the rank of rear admiral. Those not selected were encouraged to retire.

Carter felt good about his ship's performance. Flight operations had gone well. Carrier operations were always rushed and dangerous, carried out on impossibly small, moving flight decks. Accidents happen frequently. The unprecedented safety record of the Mariana Straits was known—and envied—throughout the fleet. And there was little remaining time for anything to go wrong. The seven–month deployment was drawing to a close. In just fourteen days, the Mariana Straits would secure from flight operations and leave the Tonkin Gulf. It was scheduled to sail under the Golden Gate and Bay Bridges and tie up at Naval Air Station Alameda just ten days later. Captain Carter and the Mariana Straits were now playing out the clock.

Captain Carter retired to his "at sea" cabin at 2200. As usual, he intended to return to the bridge when flight operations resumed at 0600, with the first launch scheduled for 0630. Sleep now came easily for the Old Man. Advancement to flag rank seemed like a sure bet. But that was before Lieutenant Junior Grade George Paige came off the midwatch in Main Engine Control.

At 0340 LTJG Paige climbed up the ladder from Main Engine Control. Lieutenant Branch had just relieved him as Engineering Officer of the Watch. When Paige reached the second deck—just below the hangar deck—he turned aft and walked through the aft ordnance assembly area, adjacent to the after mess deck, where dining sailors could watch aviation ordnancemen attach detonators to bombs. The mess decks were quiet at that hour, with only a few sailors seated there, half–dozing while drinking coffee.

In the adjoining ordnance assembly area, however, Paige saw two men wearing long–sleeved red t–shirts with their denim bell bottoms, furiously throwing punches. Paige yelled, "Knock it off!" The smaller man landed a left jab that rocked the larger one. Paige tried again, "Attention on deck!" The combatants belatedly noticed his khaki officer's uniform, dropped their fists, and came to a rough approximation of the position of attention.

On aircraft carriers, flight deck crewmen wear colored shirts, to aid the Air Boss and Flight Deck Bosun as they choreograph the carefully timed aircraft launches and landings. Catapult crews wear green, crewmen in purple shirts ("Grapes") fuel the aircraft. Blue shirts push the aircraft around the flight deck under the direction of officers in yellow. Those wearing red shirts move the bombs and missiles up from the magazines to the ordnance assembly areas, arm them, then move them up to the hangar and flight decks and attach them to the aircraft.

Like other flight deck crewmen, the "red shirts," (also known as "BB stackers") work at least twelve–hour shifts, under brutal pressure. Both bombs and Sidewinder missiles have been known to ignite in the assembly areas, as well as on the hangar and flight decks. Therefore, the petty officers who supervise the red shirts tend to be strict to the point of fanaticism.

LTJG Paige figured the fight would have been about a woman, a gambling debt, the honor of the great state of Texas, or something of similar consequence. The other red shirts in the area seemed to have enjoyed the dramatic relief. The few crewmen who had been drinking coffee on the mess deck had left, probably fearing something might blow up.

Paige took pride in never having been a martinet, or even much of an authority figure. He tried not to even see incidents like this. He wanted to ignore it, take a quick shower, and get three hours of heavy rack time before reporting to the Engineering Logroom at 0730. But in spite of his aversion to getting involved in disciplinary matters, two things made him stop and step in. First, the ordnance assembly areas were extremely dangerous. Catastrophes with the potential to kill hundreds of men could begin there. Secondly, one of the sailors on the mess deck might have noticed Paige's studied indifference to a gross safety violation. If a witness should report that an officer had seen the fight, but had done nothing, that officer would be in deep trouble. It might even lead to serious disciplinary action, something Paige didn't want to risk.

Not a petty officer in sight, Paige noticed as he reluctantly took charge. "Are you red shirts as dumb as you act?"

"No, Sir," the taller ordnanceman said.

"Yes, Sir," the smaller red shirt said, probably hoping to defuse the tension, and thus lower the consequences.

Paige took down their names and rates, then headed forward to the Master–at–Arms shack, located forward of the hangar deck. It took about five minutes to fill out the paperwork to put the two red shirts "on report." Paige could then finally head aft for a quick shower and a much needed rendezvous with his waiting rack. Within sixty seconds, of lifting his feet off the deck and onto his rack he was asleep, the trip to the MAA shack obviously not weighing on his mind. Less than 120 seconds later, his stateroom phone rang. Paige's roommate Tim, who had been asleep for several hours, didn't flinch.

"LTJG Paige."

"George, Lee Hamilton." Paige knew Hamilton, of course, but not well. He was a weapons officer and Paige was an engineer, so their work didn't overlap. They had occasionally talked at meals, or in port, at officers clubs. Hamilton was a former enlisted man, a "mustang" Lieutenant. Older than others of his rank, he looked and sounded more like a kindly college professor than the red shirts' boss. He even smoked a pipe.

"Yeah Lee?"

"Can we talk about my two men you just placed on report?"

Oh Hell. "Can't it wait a few hours, Lee?"

"Sorry, George. I just hoped you might be willing to withdraw the paperwork. I promise you I'll take care of my two knuckleheads. They'll be chipping paint for the next two in–port periods. They'll hate that worse than anything the Old Man could hand out at Captain's Mast."

"Lee, dammit, they were fighting in a bomb assembly area. And there was no petty officer around. If you had had a Second–Class, or even a Third–Class Aviation Ordnanceman in charge, I could have told him to place the fighters on report, and he could have gone directly to you. You could have handled it off the books."

"George, there was an AO2 in charge, but he had to go to the head."

"I don't see how I can let it go now, Lee."

"This will end the ship's record safety streak, George. And you know how proud of that record

the Captain is. We haven't had an ordnance–
related accident or incident since he's been on
board, and even for the deployment before that.
He doesn't want it to end on his watch. "

Paige knew that, of course, like everyone
else. The Old Man rarely gave a pep talk to the
crew without mentioning the Mariana Straits's
"sterling" safety record. He made sure the ship's
mimeographed newspaper, the *Furious Dragon*,
mentioned it frequently. He often spoke of it as
"his" safety record. Putting men on report for a
blatant—and dangerous—breech of ordnance–
handling regulations would end the safety
record. A negative development this noticeable,
especially so close to the end of the Mariana's
Straits's deployment, could well jeopardize the
C.O.'s chances of selection. It would come to the
notice of the Pentagon brass just as they were
finalizing their conclusions about who had earned
the rear admiral's star, and who hadn't.

"I didn't create this problem, Lee."

Hamilton said, "Captain Carter isn't going to
be happy, George, no matter who he decides to
blame."

*Wow! No more Mr. Nice Guy. Good–bye
Mr. Chips.* Paige realized that while Hamilton
wanted to sound tough and threatening, he was
obviously sweating nails. As "Weapons Boss," he
would be the ultimate and inevitable target of

the Old Man's rage. Lee had three years left until retirement; he didn't want to complete them at a weather station in the Aleutians.

At this point, there was no hope of sleep, Paige realized. It would be another fifteen or sixteen hours, at least. "Lee, those miscreant red shirts are your men, assembling your bombs, and not respecting your authority. Why the Hell should I have to do anything?

Hamilton didn't answer immediately. He finally said, "No good can come from any part of this, not for anybody. The two men you caught have been humping 500–pound bombs for four hours. A little bit of hot temper is understandable. An outstanding petty officer had to leave the scene at just the wrong minute. His record would be blemished. I need one more good duty station before retirement. The Old Man wants to be an admiral. All of us will have to live with the consequences of your decision. But you are a reservist who will be getting out of the Navy in a few months. You are the only one without a damn thing on the line. But regrettably, you are the only one with any power right now. Only the officer or petty officer who puts a man on report can pull the paper and make it go away. You are about to foul up the lives and careers of at least five men. And you will walk away without a scratch!"

"Screw you, Lee," Paige said quietly as he hung up. He sat in the dark for two or three minutes, then turned on the small reading light over his rack, so he could find the sweaty khakis he had worn on the midwatch. One tan sock took a minute to find. He doused the light and left the room quietly. Tim slept on.

Doing the right think is like volunteering. No good ever comes of it. Bad things inevitably happen. The old cliché about no good deed going unpunished is right on target. Doing the right thing doesn't set or maintain any safety records.

Paige walked all the way forward to the MAA shack and withdrew the reports he had filed half an hour before. Officially, there had been no incident in the after ordnance assembly area. *Remember, it is not personal. As we said at Officer Candidate School, "It's only part of the harassment."*

The Mariana Straits, loaded with highly explosive ordnance, jet fuel, aviation gas, and Navy Special Fuel Oil, sailed on. At 0600, the aircraft and flight deck crews made preparations for the initial launch at 0630.

Captain Carter came onto the bridge. He had slept well and was refreshed. As he surveyed the flight deck and the dozens of men in green, red, purple, blue, yellow, and brown shirts moving quickly about the flight deck, he felt even better about his chances for his admiral's star than he had the previous night.

Nothin' On Me

"Tom, you are going to give Machinist's Mate Second Class Thomas Charles the vigorous defense to which he is entitled." Commander Bates, my boss at the Subic Bay Naval Base's Judge Advocate General's office, didn't even try to suppress his sarcasm.

"Sir, I wanted to prosecute this case."

"For the last year, you've wanted nothing but the easy wins, Tom. These young JAGs who are still interested in doing their jobs don't need a sure loss. Jeff Gaines will prosecute," Commander Bates said.

He was right. I had become a blatant, obnoxious short–timer. I looked forward to the "rank" of civilian. I constantly let people know the status of my "short–timer's calendar." When I had walked into the office that morning, I had announced, "four months, one day, and counting." Jeff Gaines, to the contrary, retained the zeal of a rookie.

The Hong Kong docks can't accommodate ships the size of aircraft carriers. On Hong Kong port calls, the USS Mariana Straits, one of the Seventh Fleet's older carriers, rode at anchor two miles out. Liberty boats shuttled crew members to and from the waterfront. These boats were the obsolete craft that were once used in amphibious landings. The cox'n, who controls the boat, has a high perch, with a seat and the helm. The passengers don't even have benches. They stand in a deep well for the short runs to the shore, or the docks, if there are any.

On February 15, 1969, on a late return run to the ship, a sailor went berserk, slashing two shipmates with a straight razor. One nearly bled to death; the other suffered permanent damage to his left arm. The night was dark, the well of the boat darker, and most of the sailors were drunk. Some more, some less. Even so, more than ten men said that Machinist's Mate Second Class Thomas Charles had swung the straight razor.

Seventh Fleet headquarters decided to hold the court martial at sea, aboard the Mariana Straits, three weeks later. It was unusual to try a case on board a ship conducting combat operations, but doing so had the advantage of preventing press coverage.

When I tried to prepare his defense, my client refused to disclose any information or to assist in any way with his case. His entire contribution to his defense consisted of, "They ain't got nothin' on me." I had no choice; my only strategy had to be the creation of reasonable doubt.

Jeff Gaines, the trial counsel, or prosecutor, opened the prosecution case. He called six of the sailors who had been in the well of the liberty boat. Each said that Charles had been there, he had been drunk and abusive, and he had pushed his way toward the cutting victims. One witness even said Charles had shown him a straight razor earlier that evening.

On cross examination, I forced five of the witnesses to admit that they could not say with absolute certainty that it had been Thomas Charles who cut the two sailors. However, Electrician's Mate First Class Juan Lopez insisted he had definitely seen Charles slash the arm of the surviving victim. Lopez was a young, respected petty officer who was moving quickly up the promotion ladder. This made our defense more difficult.

"Are you absolutely certain you saw Charles, and no one else, cut the two victims?" I asked.

"Yes, sir."

"It couldn't have been any other man on that dark, crowded boat?"

"No, sir."

"Lopez, how much did you have to drink that night?"

"I'm not sure, sir."

"Six beers, maybe more?"

"Probably, sir."

"Could you have had as many as ten or twelve?"

"That would be a lot, sir."

"But you are not saying you didn't have twelve beers?"

"I can't say for sure, sir. Lopez was rattled. Good. I would ride this statement hard in my summation.

I didn't consider putting Charles on the stand, not that he would have agreed, anyhow. I was not surprised when the court–martial board, or jury, came in with its finding of "Not Guilty." Nor was I glad. Charles had damn nearly killed one man and injured another for life. But defense lawyers can't have regrets. I had given my unwanted client the defense to which he was entitled. I had shaken a credible witness; I had created doubt; I had won. I'm sure no one involved—not even the five officers on the board—seriously considered Charles innocent. Jeff, the trial counsel, had made a strong case. But he just couldn't overcome my argument for the presumption of innocence.

Three months, seven days, and counting.

After acquittal on a serious charge, the Navy routinely reassigns the accused, mainly for his protection. Seventh Fleet transferred Charles to the destroyer USS Blue, then widely known in the Seventh Fleet as the worst duty station possible for engineering personnel, due to its age and frequent breakdowns.

A couple of months later, back at Subic Bay, a routine incident report drove an icicle into my chest:

Lopez, Juan R., EM1, USS Mariana Straits, exsanguinated from incision to throat. Place of incident: Street outside Apony Bar, Yokosuka, Japan. Thomas Charles, MM2, USS Blue, taken into custody by Shore Patrol. Currently being held in Yokosuka Naval Base brig.

Unfortunately, the Mariana Straits and the Blue had steamed into Yokosuka at the same time. Charles obviously still carried a grudge, and a razor. The Shore Patrol arrested one of the men who killed EM1 Lopez. They can't get the other, the one who did his job, who beat the system, who "won."

They got nothin' on me.

Two months, eight days, and counting.

Forgotten but Not Gone

Arnie had once played a bit part in four episodes of a situation comedy. While the series had been canceled thirty years earlier, it still represented the zenith of his career. He had never secured another continuing role. This discouraged Arnie, but did not defeat him. Unlike legions of other bit–part players and has–beens, he refused to leave acting. He told all who would listen, "I'm true to my craft. I am a performer; I will always be a performer."

One of Hollywood's lesser talent agencies continued to represent Arnie, although it had long since stopped promoting him. He visited the agency every day. "That is what a professional does," he said.

Jan—the receptionist—always tried to look encouraging, or at least sympathetic, as she said, "Nothing today."

After checking in at the agency, Arnie always went to the McDonald's next door, where he nursed one cup of coffee for as long as anyone would listen to his stories. Aspiring young actors from the same agency also came there. Like Arnie, they couldn't afford the Starbucks across the street. Unlike him, they went there to kill time until the restaurants where they waited tables opened. Sometimes the newer ones listened to Arnie as he described his acting odyssey.

"At first the sit–com residuals got me through," Arnie told a couple of actress/waitresses one morning.

Sally, the more experienced of the waitresses—by virtue of a long–ago walk–on part in an episode of *Moonlighting*—said, "What did you do when they started running out?"

"Bit parts, here and there. And I've gotten a fair number of commercials."

The younger woman said, "Are there any commercials we might have seen you in?"

"I've been a pancake, a muffler, and a ballpoint pen. I've played a can of Pennzoil. Once, I was an emergency fill–in for the guy who played the apple in the Fruit–of–the–Loom commercials."

I guess I've missed them," the woman said. "I've heard commercials pay pretty well."

"And you get to act, really act," said Arnie. "I played the best pancake ever captured on film. I take commercials as seriously as any other role."

One morning, Lori Bates, a freelance reporter, visited the run–down agency next to McDonald's. She talked with a few aging actors for a nostalgia piece. Afterwards, she walked next door for coffee and to review her notes.

From an adjacent booth, she heard Arnie tell a young man, "I've always remained true to acting. I've never taken a job as a waiter, a convenience store clerk, a process server, or a substitute teacher."

When the young man left, Lori introduced herself and asked if she could join Arnie. She felt another nostalgia story shaping up—one about has–beens who barely were.

"What was your strongest, most complete role, Arnie?"

"No question about that," he said. "It was a movie, *From Campus to Quarterdeck.* I was only twenty–one. It was my only starring role."

"I don't believe I've ever heard of that one," Lori said

Arnie took a small, careful sip of his coffee. He was running low. "It was before you were born. A small production company—it's gone now—got a contract from the Navy to make a recruiting film. They wanted something to take around to colleges to promote Officer Candidate School. It came out in 1968, at the height of the Vietnam War. The Navy wasn't an easy sale on campuses then."

Without asking, Lori walked to the counter and ordered two fresh coffees. She placed one in front of Arnie. "Tell me about your role."

"The film presented two themes—tradition and opportunity. A college graduate could step off his campus, report to OCS, then receive his commission eighteen weeks later. He became an 'officer and a gentleman,' in the tradition of John Paul Jones, James Lawrence, and John F. Kennedy."

"Who was James Lawrence?" Lori said.

"He was captain of a ship that got shot up badly by the British during the War of 1812," Arnie said. "He's the guy who said, 'Don't give up the ship!' He was a true hero because of his absolute commitment."

"Oh," Lori said.

"In the film, I was the actor who made the transition from frat boy to naval officer, moving from a carefree student life to a serious, responsible position in a few quick weeks. We went to Newport, Rhode Island, and shot the film at Naval OCS. The production company filmed and recorded several of the instructors, as they worked in their classrooms, but other than that, I had the only speaking part. The real officer candidates who surrounded me in the classrooms, the mess hall, and the parade grounds didn't say anything. A narrator and I—along with a lot of march music—carried the story."

Lori caught up on her scribbling. "How did the Navy like the movie?"

"I heard later that the brass really liked the message and the production. However, it failed as a recruiting tool. In the late 1960s, patriotism and the military were unpopular on campuses. According to some recruiting officers, the college kids booed it, when they weren't laughing at it. The audience hated the best acting I ever did. And I looked good in those dress blues, too! I learned something from that short movie. The career sailors I met really impressed me. They were true to their profession."

Three weeks later, one of the aspiring actors at McDonald's showed Arnie the Entertainment section of *USA Today,* with Lori Bates's byline above an article on forgotten supporting actors. Lori quoted Arnie at length. She recounted his recruiting film story and commitment to acting.

The story conferred real celebrity among the younger people at McDonald's. They gathered at Arnie's table more often. Sometimes, a second cup of coffee mysteriously materialized in front of him, to keep the stories coming. Despite his new celebrity among the underemployed, he was never anything but brutally honest.

A singer/songwriter/busboy asked, "What was the worst job you ever had? Did you ever have to compromise?"

Arnie didn't hesitate. "I've *never* sold out. If some jobs have not strictly been acting, they always represented some form of entertainment. The worst job was last winter, in Cancun. I rode a shuttle bus between a group of outlying resort hotels and downtown, with stops at the water park, the malls, and the open–air market. I announced all the stops, in English. But my real job was to entertain the tourists, to distract them from the miserable conditions on the buses—the heat, overcrowding, the slow traffic, and so on. The driver, Willi, and I badly needed the tips. The better the jokes, the more and better the tips. Willi said I was the best announcer on any shuttle. But, boy, was that miserable work."

An actor/ weightlifter/waiter whistled softly. "A comic on a shuttle bus. That's got to be close to the lowest rung in show business."

In spite of his audience's admiration, Arnie was worried. Maintaining professional integrity was getting tough. His fortunes had declined even further since returning to California. He had had only two brief jobs. One was a thirty–second, non–speaking part as a London Bobbie in a dinner–theater mystery at a motel restaurant in Westwood. In the other, an independent film production, he actually had a line. When the protagonist—a teacher—asked her colleagues in the faculty lounge if anyone had a cell phone she could borrow, Arnie extended one and said, "Here."

He had hoped to get more commercials. With the baby boomers aging, there ought to be a lot of parts for a sixty–one year old actor—pitching Metamucil, Caribbean cruises, and burial insurance. And Buicks, of course. But nothing was happening. Morning after morning, Jan tried to look encouraging when she said, "Nothing today."

Arnie had to face it. He was going to have to find a job outside show business. But of course he had no "day job" skills. None. He had noticed that McDonalds always seemed to have an older person or two on the day shift. But he wondered if he could even handle such a job. While he probably could, he decided, he wouldn't be able to rationalize it as a performance medium. He could no longer claim integrity as a professional.

Jan, his friend from the agency, rushed in and sat down next to him. He wondered what she was doing at McDonald's. She was a Starbucks chai drinker.

"Arnie, I'm glad you're still here. You've got a job, a great job! I'm so happy for you!"

"A job?"

She nodded. "Do you remember that story Lori Bates wrote about former sitcom actors?"

"Of course," he said.

"An admiral called. He said he's in charge of something like the Navy's personnel bureau."

"The Bureau of Personnel. It must have been old BUPERS himself," Arnie said. "What could he want?"

"He said he's been trying to find you for months. He called all the talent agencies he could find a listing for. Somehow his 'yeoman' missed us. What's a yeoman?"

"A secretary," Arnie said. "Keep talking."

"He said thought you might be dead or totally out of show biz," she said. "Then he read Lori's article in *USA Today*. He called her and she referred him to the agency. I took the call."

By then, Arnie had crushed his empty cup. "So what does old BUPERS want?

"You mean Admiral Miller," Jan said. "He and the Navy want to make another recruiting film, sort of. This one will be for junior officers approaching their release date. It will present some reasons they should think about staying in, making the Navy a career. Anyhow, he wants you to star in it."

Arnie was amazed. "Do you know why? I'm pretty old for this kind of stuff."

"He said that *From Campus to Quarterdeck* changed the course of his life. Immediately after seeing it during his senior year at Cornell, he applied for Navy OCS. He said that was when he realized for the first time in his life that he wanted to lead. He found the Navy both challenging and rewarding. About a year ago, he decided to make this movie as sort of a sequel to the one you were in. And he apparently has the juice to do it."

"He sure does. BUPERS has more juice than Minute Maid. It's the department that decides where every sailor and officer goes and what kind of work he or she does. Those assignments make or break careers. Everybody is afraid of BUPERS."

Jan sipped her coffee. "Admiral Miller said that when he decided to make this movie, he knew he wanted you in it. In the first one, you were an officer candidate, and then an ensign. In this one, you will be a crusty—but philosophical—old salt, an admiral just about to retire. They'll splice pieces of the old film into the new one, cutting back and forth from you as a young officer candidate to you as a distinguished veteran of three wars."

She continued, "The only thing that concerned Admiral Miller was whether you would be recognizable as the same man when they spliced in the footage from the old film. We emailed him your latest picture and he was delighted. Oh! He said to tell you that seeing you in the officers' dress blue uniform in that recruiting film was downright inspirational. You'll wear those blues in this movie, but this time you will have a lot of gold on your sleeves."

The veteran entertainer was practically speechless. "Amazing," he said, "amazing."

Jan unzipped her purse and pulled out a handful of papers. "Admiral Miller faxed a contract. We can go over it right now, if you like."

Arnie had already pulled a pen and a five–dollar bill out of his pocket. "Gimme that contract! Get us some more coffee. Some cookies, too. We'll toast Captain James Lawrence."

Lee Harvey Oswald:
Whistle and Thump

Her silent affirmations kept the nurse from going completely insane. "We are saving a lot of them, more than have ever survived major wounds in any war." Or, "That kid will go back to his mom and dad. Life with one arm is hard, but it is life." Or, at the very worst, she told herself, "I was holding his hand; he didn't die alone, out in the mud."

From time to time, when she could depressurize enough to think about it, she understood the hollowness of her affirmations. They were futile, wishful thinking. But she rarely had time to think. The hospital was near the big Viet Cong tunnel network at Cu Chi. A fuel dump and artillery battery stood across from the hospital, making the area a frequent target. The hospital staff often heard the whistles of VC mortar rounds, followed by loud, explosive thumps.

Captain Eileen Curtis knew she was fighting off madness. And she knew she could lose. But for now, affirmations and curses kept her going. The former were inaudible; the latter were not.

Sometimes she yelled them. She frequently appealed to the almighty, "God damn Roy!" In her less rational moments, she directly blamed Roy for her presence in Vietnam, for making her treat the maimed and attend the dying. Other times, she yelled, "Damn you, Lee Harvey Oswald!" Nobody at the field hospital knew why.

A little over four years earlier, as Eileen finished a late, rushed lunch in the cafeteria at Dallas's Parkland Hospital, she barely heard a couple of doctors paged "stat." Then she heard two more doctors—neither of whom she knew— paged more clearly and urgently. She saw staff running toward the ER. Something was wrong, apparently badly wrong. It looked like some sort of mass casualty incident.

Like the rest of the staff in the cafeteria, she felt an urgent need to get back to her unit. She was on the orthopedics floor, just completing her first six months of work since graduating from the University of Texas School of Nursing, in Houston. Word began to spread that President Kennedy and Governor Connally had been shot. Nobody knew any more.

As Eileen got to her floor, three nurses and Roy, an orthopedic resident she had dated a couple of times, were in the Head Nurse's office, bending over a transistor radio.

Roy quickly reached out to hug her. "The

President has been shot! The extensions are jammed; the Secret Service has taken control of the switchboard. We can't find out what is going on." Neither Roy nor Eileen, nor the other ortho nurses became involved in the incident in any way. They were simply citizens, extremely close to the scene.

As the awful day, then the weekend progressed, the news became oppressive. Eileen cried a lot; Roy a little. He broke two pipe stems clenching his teeth. After that weekend, they became almost inseparable. Roy spent as many nights and weekends at her apartment as their schedules allowed. He was gone only duty nights and about every third weekend, when he left Dallas to cover emergency rooms in rural hospitals, something many residents did for extra income. Heavy med school debts, he told Eileen.

Two weeks before the end of his residency, he promised to take Eileen to a French restaurant they knew and enjoyed. She bought a new dress for the occasion and to celebrate the job Roy had lined up in San Diego. She did her best to fight back hopes for a diamond.

Two days before the big night, an old classmate from Houston, now working in pediatrics at Parkland, asked Eileen to go out for a drink. "You are going to hate me," Jennie said. "I know you have been getting serious about Roy. I hoped you wouldn't." Eileen just stared.

"He's married, and has been for three years. His wife and daughter live in Corpus Christi. She's a nurse anesthetist there. That's where he goes on the weekends when he leaves here. Did he tell you he's taking a job in San Diego? He's not. He's really moving back to his family in Corpus."

"Dammit, Jennie! Stop!" But Eileen realized it was true. Roy had been planning to dump her at the "special" dinner.

After crying for three days, Eileen decided to stop. "When everything comes apart where you are, go somewhere else," she told herself. It was time to leave Dallas and Parkland. The kindness and sympathy from the other ortho nurses, and especially from Jennie, were becoming tiresome and embarrassing.

Eileen still had the card of an Army recruiter who had visited her during her last year of college. She called Major Franks and asked if the army still wanted nurses. The army did. Within a month, she received a physical, a security clearance, and a direct commission as a first lieutenant. Following a short orientation to the army, she reported to Tripler Army Medical Center in Honolulu. After a year there, she received her captain's bars and orders to the 12th Evacuation Hospital in Cu Chi.

A field hospital meant olive drab fatigues instead of the Tripler's crisp whites. It meant triage, deciding quickly and ruthlessly which men might benefit from surgery and which ones had no chance. There was no finesse. "Meatball surgery": patch them up; ship them to Saigon or Cam Ranh Bay, then to Tripler or to Letterman Medical Center, at the Presidio, if they were lucky.

Trauma surgery, amputations, and death passed quickly on some days, slowly on others. Symptoms of madness were universal facts of life, like the constant shortage of dressings and the lack of suction in surgery, the excruciating pain of the troopers, and the incredible endurance of the surgeons. Movies, USO troupes, and occasional R & R trips to Saigon did not cure the madness. Chaplains didn't help. "They are as crazy as the rest of us," Eileen told the chief surgeon.

"Maybe more so," the doctor said.

Madness was a personal matter. Every surgeon, nurse, medic, orderly, and chaplain was expected to hold himself or herself together—to cope, not to whine. At Cu Chi, there was no time for—or tolerance of—personal problems.

So Eileen moved from one day to the next, relying on her silent affirmations and audible curses. On a rainy morning when a Huey came in with twenty wounded, she started the day with a loud, "God damn Roy!" She added a "God damn Lee Harvey Oswald!" They had put her here.

When the day finally quieted down, and she

had a chance to sit back for a coke and about five Marlboros, her silent affirmations held her together. "His parents will be grateful to see him. Babies will be born because we saved that sergeant's life."

It started over. A Huey came in. Surgeons changed gloves, but not masks, as they moved from amputations to abdominal stitches. Flies buzzed from one spot of blood to another. A medic fainted. A corporal slipped away as a chaplain lied, telling the boy he would go home soon. Nurses passed forceps, scalpels, and hemostats. Eileen's underwire bra dug in as she leaned over one casualty after another. She moved from a sucking chest wound to a splenectomy, almost numb, physically and mentally. The chief surgeon scratched his name on a document on a clipboard, held up by a clerk. A thoracic surgeon cursed, a PFC screamed, a nurse choked on a sob. The field telephone growled; it growled again. Nobody picked it up.

One table cleared, then another. Nurses, medics, and orderlies walked away, then removed their masks. They said nothing. The chief surgeon dropped onto a folding chair near the Quonset wall, then leaned forward to take a coke from an orderly.

Eileen told herself, "Every one of these surgeons did more good in a morning than Roy will do in a year. Every one of us matters. I matter.

The orderly swabbing up the blood matters." As usual, she made her silent affirmations to hold off insanity.

For some odd reason, Eileen thought about *Li'l Abner*, the old Al Capp comic strip. Mammy Yokum, the matriarch of the town of Dogpatch, had frequently said, "Good is better than evil, 'cause it's nicer!" The tough old lady had it right. The damnation of Lee Harvey Oswald and Roy, she realized, was less important than the children that the sergeant they had patched up would father.

That night, Eileen was gentler than usual as she made her late rounds of the casualty tent. She listened intently to each wounded man. She did not have to hold the hand of a dying soldier. Walking back to the nurses' quarters, she understood, for the first time, that she would not succumb to madness. "It was the right thing to come here." She didn't need to damn anybody any more.

She heard a whistle, but not the thump.

Temp Work

The man, rumpled and disoriented, stepped off the bus and lurched slightly as he walked to a nearby cement bench. However, as he turned to take a seat, his movements suddenly became graceful, elegant, remarkable for one so obviously hung over. He pulled a crumpled Pall Mall pack and a matchbook out of his left sock. He extracted one of the cigarettes and lighted it. His hand movements were precise and graceful. I wondered if he cleaned up well.

"Hello sir," I said. "You are a seafaring man, aren't you?"

"Screw you, Sherlock Holmes," he said. "Everybody in San Diego knows sailors keep their cigarettes in their socks. And don't call me 'sir'. I'm an Electrician's Mate First Class, not a damn officer."

"I'm sorry I offended you. I spent some time at sea myself. I used to keep my cigarettes in my sock. But then I quit smoking."

"Scared of cancer?"

"No, my wife," I said.

He snorted.

We sat without speaking for at least a minute. Then I said, "You've let me know you don't like small talk. So, could you use some work?"

"I got work, I told you. I'm on the Enterprise; we shove off for the Tonkin Gulf on Thursday."

"Just for this evening," I said. "Five hundred dollars for two hours' work, if we do it right." That got his interest.

I said I would tell him only what he had to know. My company depends upon discretion. No, make that "secrecy." If you have ever heard of paramilitary companies like "Blackwater," we are something like them. Unlike Blackwater, our name has never been seen or heard in the news media. Our operations—and our very existence— are on deep background.

We supply operatives, or "contractors," to businesses and government that need sophisticated security measures, up to and including the disappearance of troublesome individuals. Our contractors include former SEALS, Delta Force operators, and CIA agents, as well as veterans of the British Special Air Service and a few other elite commando units. In other words, they are skilled mercenaries.

Given our insistence on secrecy and professionalism, then, why was I trying to hire a graceful drunk who would soon be steaming overseas for months? And why pay him so much? While our operatives are always skilled professionals, sometimes we can use an amateur whose skills fit a specific task. When we hire amateurs, we pay them well, tell them virtually nothing, and part quickly.

We met at 1600, as I had specified. He had cleaned up well indeed. He was sober and neat, in a rented pinstriped suit, as instructed. His bearing was elegant and his movements graceful. "Your name is Paul Archer," I said. We went over his script at a Starbucks. He mastered it quickly, with minimal assistance. We drove my rental car to Chula Vista, once named by *Forbes* magazine as one of the country's most boring cities. "Why do you guys hire strangers for this job?" he said.

"It just seems to work out better," I found the house we were looking for without any trouble. When I knocked, a woman in her late fifties answered the door.

"Ma'am, my name is John Hughes; I represent CAE, Consolidated Alberta Energy. Mr. Paul Archer is with Dominion Insurers, also headquartered in Alberta." Both were shell companies, of course. "Are you Beatrice Adams?"

She placed her right hand at the base of her neck. The color drained from her face. "Are you here about Phillip?"

She invited us in. She told us she had received a telegram notifying her of her son's accidental death in a CAE installation in Indonesia. "I've been expecting you."

I recited my company's cover story. We could not tell her, of course, that Phillip had been killed in a firefight with anti–government guerillas in Central America. She cried, obviously not for the first time. When she asked for more details, I relied on the cover story, improvising as needed. As soon as she paused, it was time for my new contractor to go to work.

"Paul" opened the expensive leather briefcase I had provided him and took out two documents. "Because oil field work is inherently dangerous, CAE takes out substantial policies on all its employees through Dominion Insurers. Phillip listed you as his sole beneficiary. I have a check for you, made out for $750,000."

The amount stunned her; it almost always does in these cases. The next step was almost automatic. My "temp" unfolded the second document. "Mrs. Adams, if you will just sign this disclaimer, forfeiting any future claims of liability on the part of any corporations or governments associated with the project Phillip was working on, or of becoming a party to any future investigations, I can turn over this check and we can leave you in peace."

"Paul's" manner and bearing were those of a practiced professional. His very smoothness summoned up credibility and reassurance. He placed the disclaimer on the coffee table in front of Ms. Adams and presented her with an expensive fountain pen, already uncapped. She thanked him, then signed on the line he indicated. Like the others whose signatures I've needed on such documents, she did not notice that Dominion Insurers was not the company name on the disclaimer. Instead, this document bore my company's real name. It will be secured in our files in the event that we should ever be threatened with a government investigation.

When we got back to San Diego, I dropped my confederate off near the old Fleet Landing. I handed him an envelope containing ten one–hundred dollar bills. He counted it and thanked me for the bonus. I made him sign a cash receipt.

"I know you are curious, but the extra five hundred should help with that. You're a smart guy; you can tell we're a serious company."

He folded the bills and placed them in his right sock before exiting the car. "Damn straight, Sherlock."

Smoke Gets in Your Eyes

Lovers initially laughed off their friends' misgivings, "to think they could doubt my love..." The "lovely flame dies," but they don't realize it, because "smoke gets in your eyes." The song, and the story it tells, are part of our history.

Jerome Kern and Otto Harbach wrote "Smoke Gets in Your Eyes" for a forgotten 1933 musical. But the song was so good that everybody covered it, including Fred Astaire and Nat "King" Cole. It became a staple of all the big band "girl singers" during World War II. But unlike most of the big band songs, it did not promise a bright future and good times. "Smoke" warned of betrayal, and loss.

In 1958, the Coasters not only got the song precisely right, they defined it for all time. They nailed it! But especially for the men who went to Vietnam, who set records for seeing lovely flames die, for being blinded by the smoke, and for opening letters that began, "Dear John." Those two words quickly cleared the deceptive smoke of the "lovely flame," in the Coasters' emotional, immortal, and absolutely true version.

Other Diversions

Barnstormers' Trajectory

Fiction

"Bobbie, you better put out that cigarette before Donna catches you."

"Yeah, like Donna doesn't smoke like a chimney," Bobbie said. She dropped her third Kent of the day onto the pavement and ground it out with her right Spalding Oxford. "I wish she'd come on. We need to get on to Bentonville. We need some solid practice before tonight's game."

"Damn straight," said Charlene. "Our ball handling has been sloppy for the last couple of weeks. Our shooting's been worse. If we hadn't been playing such bad teams, we'd have lost a couple of games."

"And our hair was worse than our ball handling," said Bobbie. "We probably need to double the hair spray. I heard Donna say she was going to start buying six cases of Aqua Net at a time."

"Welcome to barnstorming, Bobbi—set shots, sloppy passing, and stiff, scratchy hair."

Charlene and Bobbi were the leading scorers on the Rolla Rockets, a touring women's team formed in imitation of the All American Redheads. The Redheads had started out in Cassville, Missouri, in 1936, and now played all over the country. As of 1967, four years into their team's lifespan, the Rockets still played all of their games in the Ozarks, or in towns within a day's drive.

The Rockets—like the Redheads—played according to men's rules, competing against pickup teams of police, teachers, lawyers, as well as church– and town–league teams. A share of the gate always went to a local charity.

All the female barnstorming teams had a gimmick, invariably related to hair. The Redheads took the court with garish red–dyed bouffant hairstyles. The Rolla Rockets wore "beehive" hairdos. The action of fast—and often rough—games demanded amazing quantities of hair spray to keep their hair standing tall. Once, after purchasing three cases of Aqua Net, Donna had said, "What the Redheads are to henna, the Rockets are to Aqua Net! I swear, I wish I owned a whole bunch of Aqua Net stock."

Donna came out of the café and unlocked the team's 1957 Chevrolet panel truck. Charlene yelled "shotgun," and ran to the passenger door. Donna turned over the engine that her husband— and team co–owner—Mel kept running like silk.

"The other girls are at the beauty shop. Thelma and her assistant are teasing out the last two right now. We should get to Bentonville around three. You girls could use some practice. We want 1967 to be our best year. A good game on Tuesday means a better gate on Wednesday and Thursday."

"You say that every night, Donna."

"It's true every night, Char."

When Donna pulled onto the highway, Charlene said, "We need to talk a little bit. Our pay was twenty–five dollars short last week. And it's impossible to eat three meals a day on two dollars and seventy–five cents. Can't you tell Mel to raise our meal allowance to about three– and–a–quarter, and to give us the twenty–five dollars you owe us?"

Donna sighed and assumed her familiar long–suffering look. "You know our crowds have been a little down lately. We're playing in some hick towns we never should have booked. But that's done. In a couple of weeks we'll be playing in Springfield, Osage Beach, and Fulton—places that have always done well for us."

Charlene wasn't ready to let go. "We've been working our butts off for you and Mel and you aren't paying us squat!"

"Char, Honey, the gates just haven't been as good this year. Last night in Hollister, we only sold 250 adult tickets. Last year we drew 325 there. There have been too many nights like that."

Bobbie chimed in. "How could we not be covering the overhead? With two hundred and fifty tickets at two–seventy–five, that should come close to seven hundred dollars."

"Six hundred eighty–seven dollars and fifty cents, Bobbie," said Donna. "But a hundred and fifty went to the hospital board. The high school charged us seventy–five dollars for their gym and locker rooms and fifteen bucks for paying the janitor to sweep and lock up. And that is before paying all of you, and your food and rooms. And don't forget the beauty shops and hair spray. I swear I'm gonna buy some Aqua Net stock."

Thelma's Chat and Curl stood on the edge of town. Donna pulled to the curb and the other members of the team—Sharon the 5'10" center, Robin, Nancy, and Mary Beth—came out holding makeup cases and small overnight bags. They arranged themselves on the two rows of bench seats and a single jump seat that Mel had bolted in for Sharon. Besides being the tallest of the Rockets, Sharon was the most striking. Her amazing ash–blonde beehive and sharply angled Star Trek–style eyebrows made her look even taller. She said, "Donna, when are you going to get a decent car for us to ride in? I hear the Redheads have custom–fitted Oldsmobile station wagons."

"How do you think we'd fit your hair into an Olds, Honey? You are the main reason we need a truck." It wasn't true, but it always worked when Sharon started bitching about the team truck.

Donna was used to complaints. The girls knew the Rockets didn't draw like the Redheads, and never would. She also knew that none of them had any particular skills beyond basketball. None had graduated from college. Hell, none of them had ever even been admitted to college. None could type. Not one even held a cosmetology license. All knew they would have to take a cut in income when they left barnstorming.

"Who are we playing tonight?" Robin said.

"The Bentonville Police Department. They'll probably have a few county sheriff's deputies, and maybe a game warden or two," Donna said.

Charlene stopped looking for a Top 40 station on the radio. "Some cops are in pretty good shape."

"Most aren't," said Donna.

Charlene said, "We were slow on the breaks and backdoor cuts last week. I'll bet all our shooting averages were off. Mine was."

Charlene, a guard, was both fast and quick, a deadeye shot, and a perfectionist. She had always wanted to be a professional athlete. In high school, she played basketball and ran sprints and relays on the girls' track team. She learned early that few women were making a living in professional sports. A handful of golfers and "amateur" tennis players taking money under the table were about it. There were no women's professional basketball leagues.

Then the All American Redheads came to town. They played according to men's rules, but put together a faster, flashier product, based on superior ball handling and shooting skills, coordination, teamwork, and conditioning. The Redheads easily outplayed the best men's team in town, the Church League Champion First Baptist Church. Entranced, Charlene suddenly had a goal.

The Redheads, and imitators like the Ozark Hillbillies and the Rolla Rockets, played wherever they could find audiences. This tended to be in small towns with little competition for the entertainment dollar. Most barnstorming teams won about eighty percent of their games, playing taller and stronger—but less well conditioned and practiced—men's teams.

The barnstorming team owners recruited the best high school and Amateur Athletic Union (AAU) team players they could find. In her junior year, Charlene attended a Redheads open tryout, even though she had not reached the minimum age to sign a contract. Her shooting and passing impressed the coaches, but the slower girls' game had not equipped her with the quick reflexes and stamina essential for the Redheads.

During her senior year, Charlene's high school coach started training her for stamina and agility. When the Rockets scheduled an open tryout in Rolla, Charlene caught a bus. She was exactly the kind of player Donna and Mel wanted. An excellent outside shooter, she made perfect passes to the other guard on backdoor cuts for easy layups. Mel and Donna gave her a one–year contract. The pay was poor and the travel awful. *But it's a shot. I won't have to be a waitress.*

In her first two years with the Rockets, Charlene improved every facet of her game. She hoped for another look from the Redheads. It didn't get any better for female athletes. She could either step up to the Redheads and make decent money, or end up as a night–shift waitress at White's Truck Stop.

Bentonville High School turned over its gym floor to the Rockets at four p.m., just as the last P.E. class finished up. The team ran through all its drills crisply and enthusiastically. Donna yelled, "Robin, Mary Beth, be sure to stretch your hamstrings well, now and at the end of practice." She hated injuries. The Rockets couldn't afford them. They travelled with only six players. One substitute, usually Nancy, had the job of giving all the starters about ten minutes' rest per half. If only five players were healthy enough to play, then Donna had to suit up and play the substitute's role. While she could still dribble and pass, her shooting eye was gone. So was her endurance. She was within shouting distance of forty, and had smoked close to two packs of Salems per day for nearly ten years. She wanted to keep her playing days behind her.

In the locker room, after a quick round of Coca-Colas and crackers, they got into their shiny red one-piece, snap-front game uniforms. Then they went to work on each other's hair, retouching the damage from practice and thoroughly fogging the locker room with Aqua Net. "You girls looked like a real team," said Donna. "That's what we've been missing for the last couple of weeks. These cops are not going to know what hit 'em."

Their sacrificial opponents, the "Bentonville Lawmen," had borrowed blue cotton gym shorts from the High School's P.E. department. They wore white strap undershirts with numbers drawn on in black marker. They nervously kidded each other as they set up lines for lay-up drills, then took random jump shots. A few looked relatively athletic, but most carried extra pounds around their waistlines. The few night shift patrolmen and jailers looked pale, even pasty. The day shift officers had finely tanned left arms.

Like all barnstorming basketball teams—male or female—the Rockets always started their show with a warm-up circle. The Harlem Globetrotters had introduced this feature back in the 1920s, making a series of intricate trick

passes to a recording of "Sweet Georgia Brown."
The Rockets had developed a unique drill.
They could not match the showmanship of the
Globetrotters; they compensated with speed,
performing to the frantic pace of "Wipeout," by
the Ventures. In the last minute of the routine,
the six of them moved three balls at top speed
simultaneously, which never failed to energize
the crowd for the tipoff.

The Lawmen's center easily beat Sharon on
the tipoff. But Charlene instantly batted the
loose ball to Robin. Mary Beth had broken for the
Rockets' basket at the tip. Robin led her perfectly
with a long, two–handed pass. Mary Beth caught
it in stride and scored on an easy layup. The
crowd yelled and clapped. Few had ever seen
girls or women play the full–court game, much
less throw a half–court pass.

The Lawmen tentatively moved the ball
toward the half–court line. Bobbie darted in on
a diagonal line, stole the ball from a bewildered
guard, then drove unimpeded to the basket and
raised the score to 4–0. Once again the police
brought the ball up carefully. A guard threw a
high pass to their center. He hurried his shot and
threw up an air ball. The Rockets recovered it
and swiftly advanced the ball the length of the
court on a series of quick, sharp passes, with no
dribbling at all. The police team sagged back to

defend their basket, so Charlene threw up a set shot from three feet outside the top of the key. In under a minute the Rockets were up 6–0.

The Rockets played according their standard game plan, which called for them to run up the score in the first quarter and to use the second quarter to show off trick shots and passes. During the half, they chugged down another Coke and added about another quarter–can each of Aqua Net to their beehives. The third quarter centered on gags and comedy bits. In the fourth, they returned to running up the score.

By the middle of the final quarter all sense of competition was gone. The home town Lawmen were winded. A couple of them started taking subtle cheap shots at the Rockets. This kind of reaction was not unusual. The women spread out and went into a stall, so that any blows would be blatantly obvious. They took only outside shots. On defense, the Rockets sagged back, encouraging their opponents to put up shots. They had the score well in hand, so a few more police points didn't matter. By then, those in the audience who weren't thinking about getting their kids to bed were anticipating a quick beer or two.

Everybody was ready for the final horn. They gave the Rockets an enthusiastic—but quick— standing ovation, then filed out. The Rockets and the cops lined up for perfunctory handshakes and the announcer thanked everyone for attending. The Rockets slipped on their cotton sweatpants and red nylon logo jackets and filed straight through the locker room to the parking lot, where Donna already had the truck running. "Great game tonight!" she said. "Good gate."

"We could have beaten the Redheads tonight," Charlene said. "Damn, we looked good! Donna, you had better get serious and get us our back pay and up our meal allowance."

Donna didn't answer. But she stopped at a Texaco station and bought two six–packs of Busch Bavarian and a bag of ice. "As soon as we get back, get your showers. Team meeting in my room in thirty minutes." After letting the players out, she drove around to the motel office and picked up the outdoor pay phone.

The players, who bunked three to a room, and had to take turns in the showers, rushed to get to Donna's room at the allotted time. Charlene led the way. "Donna said it was a good gate. Maybe we're gonna get a bonus, or at least our back pay."

The Rockets, wearing robes or kimonos, their hair in huge rollers, all opened beers and looked for a place to sit. Donna, however, wore a western shirt, jeans, and cowgirl boots. Mascara was running down her cheeks.

She spoke in an unusually soft voice. "Girls, you all played well tonight. I'm so damned proud of you all. I've never had a better bunch of basketball players. You gave those people their money's worth, not just tonight, but every night on this tour. But the gate just hasn't been what it should have been. And the schools keep squeezing us to use their gyms. I just talked to Mel. The bank turned him down for a loan that would have gotten us into the last part of the season, and hopefully some better gates. We just can't go on."

Some of the Rockets had begun to cry; all looked stupefied. Charlene quickly flared up. "You can't just say 'good–bye and good luck.' You owe us!"

Donna said, "I've got to go pick up Mel in Springfield. The bank repo'd his car." She dropped the plastic pouch onto the bed. "I'm leaving tonight's gate for you all to split. It ought to be a little over $500. I managed to get out without leaving the cut for the police charity, but the high school took their $100. There ought to be enough to get you all bus tickets wherever you need to go, and then some. God love you all. I'm gonna miss you." She started hugging her players.

Charlene shook her off. "Shit!"

"I'm sorry, Char." Donna picked up the keys to the panel truck and walked out. Charlene threw her half–empty beer can at the door as Donna closed it just in time.

"She can't just leave us here like this," Robin wailed.

"She just did," Charlene said.

Bobbie considered the matter briefly. "I guess it could be worse."

"How?" Charlene said through clenched teeth.

"What if we owned a whole bunch of stock in Aqua Net?"

The Last Studebaker

Fiction

"Dammit, W.G., I told you to keep on going straight. I said it was too early to turn left."

"God almighty, Herman, I been there before. You turn left just past where the Avants' dumpster sits on the right."

"No," Herman said, "The right left is at least a couple of miles past that dumpster."

W.G. squeezed the wheel of the last Studebaker still running in Washington County, Georgia. He threw the stick shift into reverse and gunned the engine, again. Again, the rear wheels spun and the red clay mud flew.

Herman opened the door and got out to take a look. His spectator wingtips sank into the wet clay. "You're just diggin' us deeper. "When are you going to start payin' attention,

W.G.? You take the wrong turn, go another five miles, then *finally* wonder if you might be on the wrong road. Hell, this ain't even a road; it's just ruts. Then you plow right into a mud hole

258

and get us mired up to the axels. We're gonna have to find somebody to pull us out. And it's only a half–hour to sunset. Little brother, you ain't got the brains God gave a goldfish."

"Let's stop blamin' and start getting outta here," said W.G. "Instead of flapping your gums, why don't you throw some limbs and brush down around the rear tires, so maybe I can get some traction."

Herman looked around. "Shoes are ruined, might as well. You got a hatchet in this car?"

"Nope."

"How bout a rake, a shovel, maybe a hunting knife?"

"Nope."

"W.G., you are *useless*. Mama always pampered you because you were the baby. You ain't done a lick of work since Hector was a pup."

"Well, smartass, lookee yonder." W. G. pointed to a barely visible sign nailed to a tree. That sign will tell us where we are, or at least point us in the direction to find somebody with a truck or a mule to pull us out."

"What's it say?"

"Can't read it from here," W.G. said.

Herman fumed. "Then go over where you can read it."

W.G. said, "How bout you go? Your shoes are already ruint."

"Dammit! Hangin' would be too good for you." Herman trudged through the underbrush, looked at the sign, then trudged back. He opened the door, sat down in the passenger seat, opened the glove compartment, and pulled out a half–pint of Early Times. He uncapped it, then took a long swig.

"Well," W.G. said, "what did it say?"

"Drink Orange Crush."

A Hazard to Navigation

Nonfiction

Phillip Roth's *The Great American Novel* chronicles the misfortunes of the Port Rupert Mundys, who became a baseball team without a home when their unprincipled owner leased their stadium to the government during World War II, forcing the team to play all of its games on the road. An actual professional baseball team suddenly lost its home park in the summer of 1993, a year when the Mississippi truly was mighty. Like many other people, the Quad Cities River Bandits, of the Class A Midwest League, suddenly found their workplace flooded and unusable. Aerial photographs of the sunken John O'Donnell Stadium numbered among the most dramatic images of that terrible summer.

I've watched baseball, at many levels of amateur and professional competition, in dozens of ballparks in the United States and Canada, but John O'Donnell is my favorite. In its 1931 opening, a crowd of nearly three thousand watched the Davenport Blue Sox outscore the visiting Dubuque Tigers, 7–1. Despite several renovations over the years, John O'Donnell— now, sadly, officially renamed Modern Woodmen Park—retains the look of a 1930s ballpark, with a covered, curved grandstand and bleachers down both foul lines.

I prefer sitting on the first base side of the grandstand. From there, as Yogi Berra is alleged to have said, "You can observe a lot by watching." You can look out over the third base bleachers and see engines shifting boxcars on sidings, or watch traffic crossing the Mississippi to and from Rock Island via the Centennial Bridge. Best of all are the tugs pushing improbably long rigs of cargo barges. From the same seats, downtown Davenport, perched on the side of a steep hill rising from the waterfront, looks like a miniature San Francisco in a 1940s *film noir*. With all of that—and a cold beer—you almost don't need baseball. Even if the game is dull, your time— especially on a Sunday afternoon—is well spent.

Baseball at John O'Donnell came to a sudden halt in 1993. That June, it rained almost every day in eastern Iowa, western Illinois, and points north. The muddier–than–usual, suddenly swift, Mississippi flooded the railroad yard, the parking lot, and then the outfield, the diamond, and the lower rows of seats. The ballpark was surrounded by the Mississippi. It became what the Coast Guard calls a "hazard to navigation." The river rose quickly, but took more than a month to recede. There was no more baseball in John O'Donnell that year.

In baseball, however, as in all forms of professional entertainment, the show must go on. The symmetry of the game demands it. Baseball's wonderful—and frequently obscure— statistics demand it. The same number of teams must begin and end a season. Even more importantly, professional baseball is a business. The Houston Astros, the major league affiliate of the River Bandits, could not simply call off work. Minor league clubs are called "farm teams" for good reason. The major league clubs use systems of four or five minor league franchises of varying size and quality to cultivate talent. The minor leagues—or "bush leagues"—are where the majors separate the wheat from the chaff, the sheep from the goats, the pitchers from the throwers. The Astros could not simply abandon players, managers, coaches, and various other contracted employees, and upset the personnel development and evaluation of their entire multi–team farm system. The River Bandits had to play somewhere.

The 1993 team was not burning up the league when the flood hit. Like most minor leagues, the

Midwest League divides its season into "halves," with the winners of the two halves playing a championship series. In the first half that year, most of the games were played before the flood. At the end of the first half, the Quad Cities River Bandits stood fifth of seven teams in the league's Southern Division, with a winning percentage of only .385. In the second half, after the flood, they played a few home games at one of the local high schools. A picture shows fans sitting in folding lawn chairs behind the backstop, much like Little League parents. However, like Roth's hapless Port Rupert Mundys, the River Bandits played most of their games on the road, in the parks of their competitors. The loss of their home field didn't hurt the quality of their play. In the second half, they improved to fourth in the Southern Division, with a percentage of .477.

The season closed in August, when the South Bend White Sox won the Midwest League championship. The River Bandits' players—like their counterparts on the other thirteen teams—scattered. Some expected to be called to the Astros spring training camp in February; others hoped to be; and, some knew their days in organized baseball had just ended.

The fans in Davenport, Bettendorf, Rock Island, Moline, and East Moline (oddly, the Quad Cities consists of five municipalities) knew that while their favorite players would probably not be back, their ballpark would be. In 1994, John O'Donnell Stadium would be reclaimed from the muck, spruced up, and ready for play. The boxcars, tugs and barges, and twinkling headlights on the Centennial Bridge would be back. The river that had made baseball impossible to play the preceding summer would again make their park one of the greatest places in the world to watch the game of baseball. The team would play at home again.

Low Inside Heat

Fiction

Another five–inch rainstorm rolled over the Quad Cities on July 4. The first game of a scheduled Sunday doubleheader between the home team River Bandits and the visiting Ft. Wayne Cougars ended in an instant washout in the fourth inning. The second game never started. The upper Mississippi Valley had been like this almost the entire summer of 1993. On bright, hot summer afternoons, massive clouds suddenly rolled in and opened up. Rain fell at an inch–an–hour. Then the skies cleared suddenly, in time for beautiful sunsets.

For Jordan Tull, the rainout meant another lost opportunity. He had hit a single and a triple in just four innings. Because the game didn't last the requisite five innings, his hits were washed away, erased. According to the statistics, the narrative of a ballplayer's career, he had had no hits for no at bats that day. And with Slocumb—who Tull had always hit well—scheduled to pitch the second game for Ft. Wayne, he lost a chance at another big game.

"All these rainouts are killing me," Tull said to River Bandits manager Jake Gattis. Streaks come and they go. And Jordan had a great streak going. This season he had finally begun to hit Midwest League pitching. His batting average climbed from .250 to almost .330. Thanks to five home runs over a three–game series with the Peoria Chiefs, his slugging percentage topped .480.

"Just keep getting around on those inside pitches," Gattis said.

Tull knew that his career depended on his 1993 season. He needed big numbers. He sure didn't need rain–outs. In 1992, he had struggled, ending the season with a .265 average. The California Angels, then the River Bandits' parent club, seemed set to cut him. But over the winter, the Angels pulled out of the Quad Cities and the Houston Astros took control of the River Bandits.

The Astros talked Jake Gattis into coming out of retirement to manage their new Class–A club. Gattis had a solid reputation for developing hitters. He telephoned Tull at his parents' house in Ellensburg, Washington. "The Astros always need right–handed power hitters," he said. "We're gonna give you another try, Jordy. But you need to show us what you got right out of the gate."

After catching his breath, Tull said, "Thanks, Skipper. I'll see you in spring training. And I'm going to get on that low inside heat." For many hitters, fastballs thrown low, on the inside corner of the plate—or just off it—are the toughest pitches to handle. Jordan was just learning to get his bat around on the inside fastball when the 1992 season had ended.

Over the winter, he went to the Central Washington University field house daily to work out against a pitching machine and some of the school's pitchers. "Come in low and tight at least half the time," he told the pitchers. He set the pitching machine to deliver just inside the plate, knee–level. When spring training began in Kissimmee, Florida, the Astros briefly considered moving him up to their Double–A team in Jackson, Mississippi. But they finally reassigned him , to Quad Cities.

Jordan had no illusions. By the end of summer, the River Bandits would either send him to either Jackson or Oklahoma City, or cut him loose. Class A leagues exist only to develop and judge talent. They do so quickly. A few generations ago, there had been career minor league players, men who couldn't quite get around on a fast ball, or pitch "in the black," but who compiled good statistics, pleased the fans, and helped their teams in the standings. "Those days ended back when the

Dodgers went to California," Gattis told Jordan. "Now it's up or out. Fast. You're lucky to be getting a second chance."

"I'm not gonna settle for Jackson, Skip," Jordan said. "I plan to be in Oklahoma City, playing Triple–A ball, by the end of the season.

"Good. Aim high, Jordy. And keep working on that low inside stuff."

Jordan started hitting inside pitching on opening day. And he just kept getting better. He hit well at home and on the road, especially in the small parks like Burlington and Clinton. As a bonus, his glove work improved. He was running down line drives and Texas League pop–ups that he had let drop a year earlier.

"When you hit, Jordy, everything gets better," Jake said. Of course, every manager or coach Tull had ever played for—going back to Little League—had said that. Baseball runs on its clichés.

Jordan Tull's worry about not moving up eased off. His nightmares, in which he wandered around used car lots, never finding a way out, eased off. But he knew that streaks come and go. He needed every hit he could get while he had a hot hand. To stop hitting, to fall into a serious slump, would end his life as a professional ballplayer.

Beginning in early July, the freaky storms continued to hit the area two or three times a week. The skies opened and two–to–four inches of rain fell on the soaked fields and woods of Iowa and Illinois. The Mississippi River soon topped flood stage. Rock Island, Moline, and East Moline, on the Illinois side, had long since built concrete floodwalls. But in Bettendorf and Davenport, on the Iowa side, the river quickly overflowed its banks, in spite of sandbag barriers hastily thrown up by city workers, National Guard troops, and convicts. Within a few days, John O'Donnell Stadium, Davenport's wonderful 1930s–era ballpark, and the River Bandits' venue, sat in water up to its fence tops and into the second level of the grandstand.

The River Bandits management had to figure out how to complete the season. First, they played a couple of home series at one of the local high school parks. A few fans, maybe a hundred a game, showed up with lawn chairs and coolers. With the rough infields and short fences, most of the players fattened up their batting averages and their home run counts. The total runs per game averaged almost twenty. Jordan excelled, with eight homers and eighteen total hits over a half–dozen games.

Then the team and the league changed strategies. The River Bandits became the orphans of the Midwest League, playing the remainder of the season entirely on the road, in the other teams' parks.

When the permanent road trip began, Jordan's hitting started falling off, for no apparent reason. He went zero–for–four on two straight nights in Cedar Rapids. After a decent stand in Rockford, he went hitless in four games at Kane County. His hopes rose at Beloit, where he got three hits, including a homer, in a double–header. Then the bottom fell out. He skidded into a full–blown slump.

"Skip, you gotta get me out of here," Jordan told Jake Gattis before a day game in Waterloo.

Gattis stared toward the outfield wall. "How am I going to do that"?

"The Jackson club is making a run for the pennant down there. They could use an extra bat down the stretch."

"Jordy," Gattis said, "the season ain't over here. If the Houston office wants you at Jackson, they'll tell both of us. You know how baseball works."

Tull wiped his bat handle on a tar rag. "I *do* know how it works. My average and home–run count still look okay, but they won't for long. I know I could hit if I could just get out of here. This place is depressing as Hell. Everywhere we go, nobody talks about anything but storms and the flood. Even the towns with dry ballparks have had a lot of property and crop damage. If I can't get out of here, I'm done."

Gattis was used to ballplayers becoming extremely moody when they fell into hitting slumps. He considered telling Jordan just how little most people care about baseball when their houses are floating down the Mississippi, or when the places they worked suddenly closed, maybe for good. He couldn't say that, though. Professional ball players had as much to lose as any homeowner or businessperson along the river. Indeed, those folks might be able to make a comeback when the waters receded. Struggling ballplayers probably wouldn't.

Avoiding the word "slump," Gattis said, "Streaks come and streaks go, Jordy. You just go out and play one game at a time and start the next streak. And while you're at it, move back off the plate about three or four inches. That should help you get around a little faster on inside stuff. Remember, the key is to handle that low inside heat." The best he could do was give Jordan something besides storms and failure to think about when he came to the plate.

Jordan Tull hit four–for–four—with a go-ahead homer—that night. And the storm held off until the bottom of the eighth. Jake Gattis and Jordan Tull had the same thought as Jordan's home run arced over the fence. *Maybe!*

Return to the Real World

Nonfiction

I left the U.S. Navy with mixed emotions—joy and elation. Naturally, I gave no thought to ever again working in correspondence study. The farce with the Junior Officer Training Course (JOTC) on the Coral Sea had been both silly and inconsequential. Like midwatches and General Quarters drills, the JOTC was something else to put behind and forget. About six months before my release from active duty (reserve officers don't get a discharge at this point), I decided to try to go to graduate school. I quickly learned that application to a school I had attended was easier than trying to get into a university with which I had no connection at all. So I applied for the master's program in history at the University of Georgia. For reasons I've never understood, they quickly accepted me. I immediately ceased working on the stack of applications to other schools languishing in my desk drawer.

I was released in July, 1970. In the fall, I showed up in Athens, with a new wife and a couple of months to kill. Our first order of business was to find jobs and make a little money. This was easy for Joyce, a registered nurse. Saint Mary's Hospital immediately offered her the position of head nurse on their orthopedic floor. Wherever we have moved, she has quickly found a responsible position and started contributing to the community. This was not exactly the case for me. I needed a temporary job until January, when the University would begin paying me a stipend to serve as research assistant, and—more importantly—I would begin to receive a monthly G.I. Bill educational benefits check.

I had to scrounge harder and settle for less. But, I had connections. My younger brother had worked as a City of Athens garbage man most of his undergraduate years. Because of his outstanding work he was soon moved up from an ordinary garbage pickup route to the elite Leaf and Limbs division. So good was he at this job that he won the "Sanitary Serviceman of the Month" award three times in two years. His good name and reputation immediately got me a minimum wage job picking up garbage. In less than two weeks I was promoted to Leaves and Limbs. This job was not difficult. My partner, a stoner who drove the truck, usually made time for us to watch

Gilligan's Island, which was in reruns even then. He pulled the truck around behind his house. He smoked a joint and I smoked Marlboros as we watched the fine ensemble acting, featuring Bob Denver and Jim Backus.

I got another job, selling Christmas trees and ornaments at Sears, which anchored Athens's largest strip mall. As time passed they wanted more hours from their part–timers. Since Sears paid twenty–five cents an hour more than the Sanitation Department, I regretfully left Leaves and Limbs and worked forty hours plus at Sears. I did not really miss Gilligan's Island, but I did— and do—regret that I was never named Sanitary Serviceman of the Month. I was sure to have received it soon and it would have looked good on my *curriculum vita* when I finally started looking for a job teaching history.

In early January I left Sears to begin my first quarter in the graduate history program. I didn't know it then, but a few years later, I would scrounge for a few more bucks by working in the University's correspondence program. I was not proud.

Like almost all new master's program students in the History Department, I was assigned work as a research assistant (RA) to one of the professors. We were all paid a stipend that ranged between "pitiful" and "miserly." Besides teaching us about the nature of archival historical research, the RA positions gave us a way of learning just what weird individuals history professors could be.

The first of three professors I did research for, Dr. Gorski, greeted me by saying, "I've heard that you think no significant work can be demanded of graduate research assistants. Well that is wrong! You will find out that working for me is demanding. You may now think that this assistantship is a sinecure, but it is not! I will not tolerate being shortchanged. I will speak to the graduate coordinator immediately if you try to slack off on me."

Welcome to graduate school!

I decided not to try to reason with him. I had just spent three years in the Seventh Fleet. I was used to blowhards trying to throw their weight around. I certainly was not impressed. I walked down the hall to the office of the History Department's Graduate Study Coordinator, who I had not yet met. To my surprise, Jim Buck was a retired Air Force colonel, with a Ph.D. in Japanese history. I told him my story, making it clear that I had never said any of the things Dr. Gorski said he had heard about me, and that I didn't think working with him could be productive for either of us.

"Between the Fall and Winter quarters we admitted our biggest class ever," he said. "Twenty–

five new MA students. Ten of you are recently discharged veterans. In the Fall quarter some of our professors found the situation unpleasant, not to their liking. You vets don't show the kind of deference many of our older professors are used to. You don't intimidate easily. And some of our younger professors were deferment–grubbers and downright draft dodgers. Some of them consider themselves morally superior to you because they didn't participate in the war; others are just afraid of you."

"Dr. Buck," I said, "There is no need for the faculty to worry about us or to treat us differently. Most of us who did go to Nam, or elsewhere in the Pacific, are—at best—highly ambivalent about the war. I don't think any of us want to refight it."

"Yeah," he said, "and the faculty will learn that. But on the other hand, you guys have already started to change the culture here. And they won't get over that easily." He took a long drag from a Pall Mall and added, "Nor should they." He stubbed out his cigarette. "Mr. Pittman, you are not going to have to work for Dr. Gorski. I'll switch you to somebody else. Do you know Dr. Raven?"

"No," I said.

"I think you'll get along fine," Dr. Buck said. He's a nice guy. But you probably will never agree about the war. He was—and is—one of those professors who can be counted on to show up at every demonstration and teach–in. He wants to be a "hero–prof." But I don't think he will give you any crap." And he did not. Charles Raven and I had a good working relationship for the remainder of my first year.

Squelching the Smart–Ass

Nonfiction

"I didn't enroll in this course to spend ten weeks answering highly personal questions on useless questionnaires. The College of Education doesn't need to know how many siblings I have, and whether each of us had our own rooms. It is none of your business how many divorces my parents had between them. I'm willing to do whatever serious assignments this course calls for, but I'm not going to keep feeding your nosiness about my family life."

I had stayed after class to register my discontent. On the first class day Miss Whitaker had briefly introduced herself, told us we would enjoy the class, and dismissed us early. That was exactly what I had wanted. But on the following four days, we filled out questionnaires. Many of them would eventually become the basis of College of Education master's theses, doctoral dissertations, and even faculty articles.

"You and your colleagues do not need to know how many bathrooms there were in the house I grew up in," I said. Having had my say, I dropped my cigarette on the floor and ground it out with my heel, dramatically, I hoped. But Miss Whitaker did not seem impressed.

I once again began to wonder about my strategy. Back in the late 1960s, all seniors had to have a strategy. Eastern State University had devised a scheme to relieve students of just a little more tuition money in their final year. ESU was one of few major universities still clinging to the quarter—rather than semester—system. A full course load consisted of fifteen quarter hours. Over four years (summers excluded) that amounted to 180 quarter hours. But all undergraduate degrees required *185* hours. Thus, in order to graduate in June of their fourth year, students could had to graduate "on time" either take a course during summer session somewhere along the way, or by "overloading," which meant taking twenty hours or more in a single quarter.

I began my senior year knowing that I would have to overload. I decided to wait until winter quarter, when the social load was usually lighter. So I registered for twenty Winter Quarter hours. Ten hours were in history, my major. I knew they would demand a great deal of reading and writing. And I needed A's. An anthropology

280

course entitled "The African Peoples" accounted for five more hours. It sounded interesting, but I didn't know how much work to expect there.

I had devised a clever scheme—I thought—to pick up the five overload hours. Like most pseudo–intellectuals of the day, I scorned the College of Education. We College of Liberal Arts snobs believed that Education courses had no rigor, and demanded no effort beyond staying awake. How else could many of the ESU girls hope to graduate at all? I had briefly dated a couple of girls who fit the Education Major stereotype. Both spent more time thinking about flatware patterns than completing a degree.

The nickname for easy courses used to be "cripples" or "crips." I needed a crip with the least possible quantities of reading and writing. I enrolled in the most generic–sounding course the College of ED offered at the junior/senior level, *Introduction to Professional Development*. Its catalogue description was every bit as vague and pretentious as its title. I had faith—and hope—that that it would be devoid of both content and effort.

In five–hour classes, students attended class five days a week for ten weeks. My Calvinist upbringing had created its intended sense of guilt. In spite of all of my many academic sins, I never cut classes, unlike my all–female College of Ed classmates, several of whom cut two classes the first week. I dutifully went to class and filled out two or three survey questionnaires daily. Miss Whitaker assured us that we would not be graded on our responses to the surveys. "You are just sort of testing the tests," she said. In other words, the College of Ed was using us to test the validity and reliability of the survey items. Just as the Psych department used freshman as guinea pigs, the College of Ed used aspiring teachers as junior varsity "respondents."

In all respects, *Introduction to Professional Development* looked like the perfect crip. The surveys demanded no effort. The reading assignments, as listed on a simplistic syllabus, were not demanding. Indeed, it seemed safe to assume there would be no need to bother with reading them. The course was content–free. However, the daily surveys looked troublesome. Besides being a pseudo–intellectual, I was also a pseudo–liberal. Some of the questions were, I believed, unduly and unjustifiably intrusive. In a fit of righteous indignation, I decided that the students and faculty who were drafting the surveys were asking for information to which they had no right, such as, "Between them, how many times have your parents and/or step–parents been divorced?

I told Miss Whitaker all of this in our Friday afternoon conversation, as I gestured grandly with my cigarette. In a parting shot, I told her how low the College of Ed and its faculty were in the campus pecking order. This turned out to be the most foolish high horse I had mounted in my life.

Over the weekend, I spent most of my time boasting about how "I stood up to those idiots in the College of Ed." I bragged to my roommates, friends, and girlfriend that I had defended the civil liberties of everybody in the class. My eloquent refusal to permit the violation of our privacy and our civil rights, I pontificated, had bewildered the pimply Miss Whitaker. "Those questions don't belong in an academic class," I assured all who would listen. "But of course Education courses aren't really academic." My girlfriend, a German major, seemed especially impressed by my bluster. I believe a case of Falstaff beer was involved in my blowhard, often repeated defense of the First Amendment that weekend. But I could be wrong. It might have been Pabst Blue Ribbon.

On Monday, Miss Whitaker caught me as I entered the classroom. "Dr. Sawyer, the associate dean, would like to talk with you," she said. "I believe he is in his office now, waiting for you." He was indeed.

"Mr. Pittman," this august personage said, "Miss Whitaker told me that you disagree with the way she is teaching her class. And I see you are not an education major. *Introduction to Professional Development* is for young people who plan on entering the teaching profession. Why did you take this course you obviously despise, Mr. Pittman."

Why quit now? "I'll be frank Dr. Sawyer. I had to overload this quarter in order to graduate in June. I have a tough load of legitimate academic courses with a great deal of assigned reading this quarter. I'm overloading, so I badly needed a 'crip course'."

I have to give Associate Dean Sawyer credit. He remained calm and unruffled. "The Dean and I have talked over your situation," he said. "Both of us wonder how you were approved for enrollment in one of our courses." Our faculty is hard pressed. We have a difficult time serving our own students. We do not have the surplus capacity to teach students from the University's other colleges."

This was obviously false. If I had not said anything to Miss Whitaker, I would have finished the course without placing any additional strain on the Education faculty. I offered a clever retort. "Don't Education majors take courses from the College of Arts and Sciences?"

"Of course," Sawyer said. "But providing survey courses to all students is part of the mission of the College of Arts and Sciences. The mission of the College of Education is to prepare aspiring teachers. That is especially true for *Introduction to Professional Development*." He refrained from saying that students who considered their curriculum a joke were especially unwelcome.

Samuel Johnson's warning that patriotism is the last refuge of a scoundrel is outdated. Hiding behind mission statements is the *true* last refuge of modern scoundrels. But of course Dr. Johnson never heard of a mission statement. And I was sure Dr. Sawyer had never heard of Samuel Johnson.

"But I'm enrolled and have already attended a week's worth of classes. The 'drop–add' period has ended. It's too late for me to switch to another class."

"Maybe you can find a way," he said. "We have already disenrolled you from our course." I could see there was no use arguing; I had to find a course, *pronto*.

After finding and talking with a couple of flunkeys in the office of the Dean of Arts and Sciences, I learned—much to my surprise—that Dr. Sawyer did indeed have the authority to eject me from a College of Education course.

"I have to replace that course. I don't want to overload Spring Quarter; that will be my last quarter at ESU. I need a course now," I told an assistant to the Associate Dean of Arts and Sciences.

"If you can find a faculty member who will allow you to start his course this late, and if you can get the right signatures by 5:00 today, we can enroll you." I could think of two professors whose classes I had really liked, who seemed like really good guys, both friendly and interesting. One was a philosopher, the other a historian. The Philosophy Department was uphill from Arts and Sciences, History downhill. I chose the latter. Professor Roger Nichols, an extremely nice man, snorted at the unjust attitude and actions of the College of Education. He allowed me to join his class on the Trans–Mississippi West.

Problem solved. I rushed between all the offices where I had to gather signatures and managed to file all of the paperwork with most of an hour to spare. I would carry twenty quarter hours and be on track for June graduation. This solution, however, created other problems. All three history courses had brutal reading lists, as did the anthropology course. Dr. Nichols demanded about twice the reading he had required in the first course I took with him. In terms of work demanded, I would call the anthropology course about average.

That winter I had to work, harder than I had since I had finally cleared the math requirement early in my junior year. I read continuously. I pulled the last three all–nighters of my college career. My girlfriend and I had begun to get pretty serious. Indeed, she would soon become my first fiancée. But my very limited leisure time increasingly annoyed her. I felt lucky we made it through that term together.

I found myself considerably less interested in asserting my civil liberties, or anyone else's. I learned a great deal about the tradeoff between ideals and self–interest, and about when to keep my mouth shut. Finally, I realized that Miss Whitaker had said very little when I tried to bait her. She didn't get mad; she got even.

Deary Doubles

Nonfiction

The catcher—more than 200 feet away—heard my right fibula snap. So did everyone else as I slipped on wet grass, running for a deep drive just inside the left field line. After x–rays in the local emergency room, the doctor asked if I had someone to drive me the 180 miles from Ellensburg, Washington, where we had been visiting friends, and I was filling in on a local team in a softball tournament, to my home in Pullman.

"My wife is with me," I said.

"Then go home; keep some ice on the ankle as best you can in the car. Tomorrow, go to your doctor for a cast," he said.

On the drive home, I sat with my back against the left rear door, with my foot propped on a bag of dirty clothes pushed against the right rear door. Most of the road was in excellent shape, so the worst pain came from Joyce's cheerful sarcasm. "Little boys never grow up. You can't just play kids' games; you have to take them seriously.

Couldn't you just let a fly ball drop once in a while?"

After not much of a night's sleep, Joyce drove me to the doctors' office where she worked as a nurse. "Dr. Shuey will be here in just a couple of minutes," said Janey, the other office nurse. "He's not moving very quickly today," she said with a giggle.

About five minutes later, Dean Shuey, my doctor and friend, hobbled in wearing a walking cast on his right leg.

"Don't ask," he said, looking at my x–rays on the lightboard. "League softball. Stretching a single into a double with a hard slide. What happened to you?"

I described my heroic attempt to run down the deep line drive. We could hear Joyce and Janey laughing out in the hall.

Dean said, "When it comes to sports, American men are nuts. Given a choice between risking injury or easing up a little, the middle–aged male will always go for the glory, no matter how insignificant the game. I'm living proof."

Dean didn't know the half of it. I had spent most of that summer in pursuit of athletic glory.

Pullman, Washington, is a small town that houses a large university. It sits against the border of the Idaho panhandle, in a fertile wheat– and soybean–growing region known as the Palouse.

As soon as I began my first job after grad school at Washington State University, I started entering local tennis tournaments in Pullman and in Moscow, the home of the University of Idaho, just across the state line. And I got my butt kicked in a series of first–round eliminations.

I decided to set my sights lower. Most of the little towns in the Palouse and in the neighboring forests of the Idaho panhandle held summer festivals that included sidewalk sales, arts and crafts shows, cheap beer and hamburgers in the park, and often a five– or ten–kilometer run. Some of them offered tennis tournaments, usually doubles only.

I started with "Deary Days," in Deary, Idaho. At the last minute, a friend who had agreed to be my doubles partner begged off. His desire for athletic greatness obviously fell short of mine. I decided to drive to Deary anyhow. Maybe I could pick up a partner once I got there.

Everyone I met at the Deary High School tennis courts was nice, but surprised that anyone would drive forty miles just for their little tournament. The lady in charge pointed out a young guy named Roy and suggested that I talk to him. He had come just to watch a couple of friends play. I asked him if he would partner with me. He said he had played in high school a couple of years earlier, but only once since. However, he agreed to try it.

290

Roy proved remarkably steady for someone who hadn't played recently, and I had an excellent day. We easily won two rounds before we ran into the high school basketball coach paired with one of his students in the final match. They were just too good for us. But I was elated. A second–place finish in a tournament—even one so obscure— represented a personal best. Roy, pleased with his own surprisingly good play, asked if I'd like to try it again in two weeks, in the Elk River Days tournament. While I had never even heard of Elk River, I immediately agreed.

Elk River is a former Potlatch Corporation sawmill town up in the wooded Idaho hills to the east of the Palouse. It was the site of the country's first all–electric sawmill, installed in the 1920s. Its leading tourist attraction is its pet cemetery marked with a cross celebrating the resting place of a beloved dog named "Shithead Abell."

By the time I pulled into town two weeks later, I was thinking victory. Elk River claimed just over 300 residents, none of whom were high school coaches. A post in the center of the town square read, "Highway 8 Ends Here." The road into town was the only road out. Two asphalt tennis courts with faded lines and ratty looking nets stood on the uphill side of the square.

I got bad news. Roy wasn't there. It seemed he had gotten drunk the night before and cut his right hand severely while slamming it through the glass door of a tavern. He had spent the night in the Moscow jail and it wasn't clear if he was out yet. Even so, Roy had heroically gotten word to his older brother Kevin that he was obligated to find me a doubles partner. Kevin couldn't find anyone else, so he dutifully showed up himself. He warned me that he hadn't played in five or six years.

As had been the case in Deary, Elk River's tournament offered only doubles. The field was small; there were no divisions like men's, women's, or mixed. Any doubles team could enter. In the first round, Kevin and I barely managed to beat a twelve-year-old boy and his grandmother. She was tough!

In the second round, we encountered a pair of lumberjacks. They played in jeans, shirts with the sleeves torn out, and ventilated caps—one John Deere, one Potlatch Corporation. Both had beards; one wore work boots. One balanced the racket in his right hand with a can of Miller High Life in his left, putting the latter down only when it was his turn to serve. Suddenly, I couldn't get a first serve in, nor many second ones. Kevin played about like you would expect of someone who hadn't hit a tennis ball in half a decade. The lumberjacks were free swingers who often hit balls to the back fence on the fly. Yet they managed to slam just enough balls between the lines to nip us in three sets.

To this day, that second–place finish in the Deary Doubles remains the height of my athletic glory. But because neither the *Moscow Idahoan* nor the *Lewiston Tribune*—the only newspapers within forty miles—printed the results, the acclaim that Roy and I earned has been lost to sports history.

My ankle healed, of course, and Dr. Shuey cut off the cast. But his reflections on glory stayed with me. It's been more than thirty years now, but I haven't picked up a tennis racket or a softball bat since.

A Thirst in Prague

Nonfiction

The Museum of Communism in Prague is a compromise between a tourist trap and a serious effort to leave a record of a drab and poor period. Located just off the busy shopping street Na Prikope, a few short blocks off Wenceslas Square, the museum is above a McDonald's and adjacent to a casino.

The entrance and ticket–purchasing area were dusty and shabby. The carpets were worn and frayed, the walls were smudged, and Lenin's statue needed a vigorous Pledge rub–down. I haven't figured out whether the rundown look was part of an attempt to recreate an authentic Soviet satellite atmosphere or a consequence of the museum's capitalist owners keeping the operating budget down.

As Joyce and I proceeded down a hallway and into the first exhibition room, I noticed a persistent theme. The artifacts were ordinary, even mundane. However, the annotations, or "texts"—in five languages—that commented on them were excellent, as were many of the photographs. In the first room, the texts explained the international politics between 1945 and 1948 that provided the context that allowed the Soviet Union to impose its own puppet government on Czechoslovakia. Because I was initially educated as a Cold War scholar, the historical background that now seems so obscure came as no surprise. However, the critical treatment of the events and personalities went well beyond my knowledge of the era.

Before we could enter the second room, we ran into another relic of the Soviet–dominated period. An old woman at a tiny desk demanded our tickets. Since we had already been in the museum for ten minutes and seen a fair share of the exhibits, this step was clearly superfluous, as was the person conducting it. But of course that is what the Soviet period had been like. The government had created tens of thousands of useless, meaningless jobs like this woman's.

Upon presenting our tickets we were allowed to advance into the museum's other rooms. Cheap–looking bicycles and motor scooters, along with posters advertising them, dominated the commercial and industrial artifacts. These vehicles also could have profited from contact with a dust cloth and Pledge.

A recreation of an "interrogation room" looked like the dusty, but orderly office of a low–level career government employee charged with little work and less authority. Paper records and boxes of file cards underscored the anonymous, yet terrifying operations of the Soviet–dominated and trained security forces. The atmosphere was less one of terror than of a banal, bureaucratic threat, with a small—but ever–present—risk of danger.

An impressive selection of propaganda posters graced the museum's walls, seemingly at random. My favorite—or perhaps I should say most appalling—poster featured a woman in a North Korean military uniform, *circa* 1951. She protected a child from the evil forces of the United States and demanded that her country's population join her.

The best exhibit came near the end. In a small room, a random assortment of kitchen and folding chairs faced an old–fashioned television playing a documentary film in a continuous loop. The voices were in Czech, with English subtitles. The film recounted the two anti–Soviet upheavals of the Cold War period. In 1968, Leonid Brezhnev sent in Soviet and satellite troops and tanks to obliterate the "Prague Spring," promoted by Czech Prime Minister Alexander Dubcek. Several hundred people died as a result. In November and December of 1989, Mikhail Gorbachev did not send in troops when protestors faced down the decaying authority of the Soviet Union, the "velvet revolution" prevailed, and the Czechs created a government headed by playwright Vaclav Havel.

Much of the footage of this documentary had been shot in Wenceslas Square. It was remarkable to see earth–shaking events taking place on streets we had walked, shopped, and eaten lunch along just half–an–hour earlier.

I tried to find a good souvenir in the museum's gift shop. Nothing seemed right. The postcards with portraits of Lenin, Stalin, and an occasional Czech stooge were too grim, too real. The t–shirts were either too dopey or too bombastic. The key rings with reproductions of propaganda posters were not funny. At the moment, communism didn't seem funny. It was beyond satire. Even the postcard of Lenin with a red, white, and blue Mohawk seemed lacking in humor.

We left the museum for the nearest bar. The dust pervading the museum had raised a severe thirst. One of Prague's superb pilsners solved the problem immediately. No postcard or souvenir t–shirt could be as satisfying.

Soulful Reassurances

Nonfiction

The temperature in Washington Square Park was in the sixties, with low humidity. The leaves were turning; the sidewalks were dappled in the late afternoon sun. Residents of the Village let their dogs exercise in the runs. Hustlers played slam chess on the concrete tables. No doubt small, discreet transactions involving illicit pharmaceutical products were taking place here and there. It was a normal Saturday in the park until I looked up. The two huge towers that had always shown me south, from any part of Manhattan, weren't there. The feeling of fury and loss returned. This entire visit to New York was like that—normal street life one minute, cruel reminders the next.

Joyce and I had made a snap decision to come to New York. On the phone, our son seemed better. But he was still shaken, as he had every right to be. That beautiful September morning three weeks earlier had come on only his fourth day at

Carter, Ledyard, and Milburn, a Wall Street law firm. As he walked out of the subway station at Broad and Wall, the second plane crashed into the south tower of the World Trade Center. He did not yet know about the first. Not knowing what else to do, he went to his firm's office at Number 2 Wall Street. Shortly thereafter, the police cleared the building. Dan joined thousands of other New Yorkers and commuters and walked north.

We talked on the phone every night for the next two weeks. But that wasn't good enough. We—especially Joyce—needed to get our hands on him. On Thursday, September 27, I impulsively made airline reservations and booked a room at a Courtyard in Times Square.

We arrived at the hotel about 7:00 p.m., still rush hour on a Friday in Manhattan. Dan was waiting on the sidewalk. He was ready to see us; we were ready to see him. He took us to an old, famous, and expensive restaurant, the Oak Room at the Plaza Hotel. In normal times, this would have been a celebration: our newly employed son was taking us out to a great restaurant. But the room clearly wasn't itself that night. About a third filled, it was quiet, almost gloomy. The waiter was attentive, but subdued. The food was good, but we didn't do it justice. As we finished dinner and ordered coffee, we began talking about the things we had so far avoided.

"When did you first find out what had happened?"

"I heard the explosion and the sky immediately filled with paper. I saw a shoe in the street along with all the paper. A foot was still in it."

"Did you see people jump?"

"Oh, yeah."

We talked in painful detail. We learned that he was still having bad dreams. The conversation was grim, but absolutely necessary.

The next morning, Joyce and I went to the block of 47th street between 5th and 6th Avenues, the "diamond district." We had never seen it so quiet. Terrorism had apparently meant rough times.

We walked the entire forty blocks south to Dan's apartment. American flags half the size of a tennis court were suspended on cables above 5th Avenue. Street vendors sold flags of all sizes, along with t–shirts bearing Osama Bin Laden's picture and the wording, "Dead, Not Alive." Many of the small stores in Greenwich Village displayed American flag posters with the pugnacious message, "With Liberty and Justice for All. You Got a Problem With That?"

We ate lunch at a Lower East Side institution, Katz's Deli on Houston. Unlike the Oak Room, it was packed, noisy, and thoroughly normal, and thus reassuring. But afterwards, as we wandered through the East Village, I spotted another wrenching reminder of the recent horror—a crude, tattered handbill taped to a lamp post. It bore a picture of a young woman and asked if anyone had seen her. A couple of weeks earlier, queries like this one had been posted all over lower Manhattan. Those that remained were heart–breaking.

On Waverly Place, a young man in a Greek fisherman's cap, a flannel shirt, and jeans played cello. His style was intricate and soulful, but not mournful. I stopped and listened while Joyce and Dan proceeded ahead. After a minute or two, the cellist stopped playing and stood up.

I told him that I enjoyed his work, but had no idea of who he had been playing; I couldn't even take a guess. He smiled and said, "That's because it's my own work." As we talked, I picked up a CD from a stack resting on his cello case. His name was Peter Lewy; the album was *Now and Then*, a collection of his own compositions and improvisations, with the exception of Bach's "Suite Number One for Unaccompanied Cello."

"Even that one has more of me than Bach in it," he said. I handed over $15. He pointed out his email address on the CD insert and asked me to let him know what I thought of the album.

At about seven, we proceeded to Cornelia Street. Only a block long, Cornelia Street is the

hypotenuse of a triangle formed by 6th Avenue
and Bleeker Street. As soon as you turn the
corner off 6th, the traffic noise subsides. There
are actually trees. The only businesses are a
handful of small restaurants. All are good. We
walked into Little Havana, a tiny place with only
five tables for four, and two for two. A man with
a shaved head, dressed in black, asked if we had
reservations. We said, "no." He made a show of
consulting his reservations diary.

"This way," he said, snapping his book shut.
Very New York. He led us to one of the three
empty tables, handed us menus, and took drink
orders. The food was excellent, as it always is
there—black beans, shrimp flavored with lime
juice, plantains, yucca, rice. We talked about
the day. Dan told us there were lawyers in some
downtown firms who had not yet been able—
psychologically—to return to their offices. They
knew they were risking their careers, but were
unable to go all the way downtown. He, himself,
had not yet been able to visit Ground Zero.

After dinner on a pleasant evening, the
small, specialized bakeries, coffee shops, bars,
and galleries can make walking around in the
Village seem exotic. But a fire station returned
us to reality. Votive candles took up half the
sidewalk. Children's drawings were taped to the
walls. A corkboard stood on an easel. Five men

in dress uniforms—those this station had lost on Nine–Eleven—smiled at us from black and white photos. The firefighters on duty went about their chores, talking in normal voices, doing their best to pay no attention to the little knots of people who stopped and spoke in whispers.

On Sunday, our last day, we headed up Broadway. As always, street vendors with counterfeit purses and watches worked every corner. In a café on 8th Avenue. a group of young men wearing black tights, doublets, and capes with red trim tuned guitars and mandolins, while conversing in Spanish. Embroidered scarlet crests on their costumes read "Fire Department; City of Madrid." Their ensemble had come to honor their brother firefighters.

Whenever we go to New York, we try to see a musical. When we arrived at the New Amsterdam Theater on West 42nd Street, to see *The Lion King*, we found news crews, lights, and cameras. Obviously, they were not there to greet tourists. Governor Pataki had decided to join us. His public relations people had decided it would be a good idea to publicize the point that Broadway was open for business. We did not see the governor; we do not know how long he stayed, or if he liked the show.

We took a cab back down to "Alphabet City," a neighborhood bordering the East Village, to a restaurant near Dan's apartment. Radio Perfecto was one of those restaurants that opens, is briefly fashionable, then goes into decline. That September it was still trendy. A display of brightly colored plastic radios from the 1950s carried the theme. The food, however, was unremarkable. Or maybe it was just our mood. We knew we soon had to say good–bye, in a way we had never said it before. Our son was now a New Yorker, coping with living in a city that had recently been a war zone and might well be one again.

Early the next morning we headed for LaGuardia, then back to our real lives in Missouri. Dan took the subway to Broad and Wall.

Now and Then, the CD I bought on a sad, beautiful afternoon in New York, still moves me. Peter Lewy's complex solo cello pieces keep alive memories of a strange, painful, reassuring, and necessary visit.

Fun In Gotham

Fiction

Edwin spotted them the moment he stepped off the train. New York's gaudiest tabloids, stacked in adjacent racks, competed to promote maximum panic. "Dow Crashes 504 Points," in a huge font, covered three–quarters of the front page of Rupert Murdoch's *New York Post*. Mort Zuckerman's *Daily News*, shouted "Shock Market," over a picture of a Stock Exchange floor trader in a royal blue blazer, holding one hand in the air and clamping the other over his forehead. Monday, September 15, 2008, had been a bad day on Wall Street. Tuesday, September 16, promised to be another one.

"Some people go to Beirut or Kabul on their vacations; we came to Manhattan during a financial meltdown, Edwin said to his wife Candy. "Kabul might have been more fun." He gave the Pakistani inside the newsstand two bucks and took both papers. "Souvenirs, if nothing else." They walked up the subway station's stairs to

the corner of Broad and Wall. Edwin steered
Candy into a Dean and Deluca for an espresso
or two and a latte while they read the papers.
"Desperate times call for strong coffee."

"We've always had great timing, said Candy.
"We moved to Washington State just in time for
Mt. St. Helen's to dump six inches of ash on our
house. And then our house in Davenport was in
the wrong spot during the Flood of '93. And of
course our daughter was here on Nine Eleven.

From a stool at the window, they could see
camera crews and street reporters preparing for
stand–ups. "Maybe they want to get some action
shots of brokers and traders jumping out of high
windows," said Candy.

Edwin turned to page two of the *Post*. "I think
that went out with the Crash of '29. I believe
they just OD on cocaine now."

Candy couldn't concentrate on the *Daily
News*. "Well, this is a city that really knows how
to have a crisis. All those poor people on Sunday
night . . . ."

Two nights earlier they had walked by the
Lehman Building, on 7th Avenue, just north of
Times Square. At 10:00 p.m. it was still fully
lighted. From across 7th, Edwin and Candy
watched men and women in very casual clothes—
shorts and flip–flops—leaving the building, alone
or in pairs. Now former employees of Lehman

Brothers, they carried small items—lamps, cushions, plants, and most often, a cardboard box. Their stuff." Many paused briefly to talk with each other. Some hugged.

When Candy and Edwin turned on the 11:00 news that night, they saw stand–ups that had been recorded earlier, as larger numbers of laid–off "financial services professionals," cardboard boxes in hand, left the Lehman Building. Those who agreed to talk with the news crews seemed either resigned or dazed. None seemed hopeful; none appeared angry.

Edwin and Candy had spent most of Monday—day one of the crash—at the Metropolitan Museum of Art and the Guggenheim, spots where there was no shortage of tourists. Panic or no panic, the swarms of visitors had long to–do lists and limited time to complete them. With the museums, then tickets for Spamalot in the evening, Edwin and Candy resolutely kept the bad news at bay.

Tuesday morning, in spite of the gloom, they decided to go to the financial district. They had been coming to New York for the last dozen years, in either the fall or spring. Their daughter Keeler had attended the Stern School of Business at New York University, and then moved directly into a major public relations firm in Midtown. Candy and Edwin bought a time–share unit near Columbus Circle to use when visiting her.

The Nine–Eleven attack terrified them, even though Keeler neither lived nor worked in the financial district. On all their subsequent trips to New York, they visited Ground Zero and stood silently for a few minutes, in sadness and anger.

Over the years they had first visited the obvious tourist attractions, then the less obvious ones. In recent trips, they had begun seeking out more obscure spots, like the "old" St. Patrick's Cathedral, in Soho, and the Tenement Museum, on Orchard Street. Edwin had done a little research, then gradually located and photographed the sites of almost a dozen Mafia hits.

The two small college professors, if pressed, would concede that they were tourists. However, they considered themselves a good deal more sophisticated than the usual run of visitors. Candy, for example, would never have even considered visiting the outdoor set of the *Today* show to gawk at Meredith Vieira and Matt Lauer. "Why, I'd rather die!" she told friends, trying to impress them with her sophistication.

Upon leaving the coffee shop, Candy said, "This financial crisis is no joke. Yesterday was awful; today looks just as bad. It isn't even 10:00 yet, and we've probably lost tens—maybe even hundreds—of thousands of dollars in our retirement accounts. Thank God TIAA–CREF is one of the most conservative funds there is! It has taken a lot of crap for not grabbing at high–growth equities. But that should pay off for us now." After a pause, she added, "I hope."

Out on the sidewalk, the fourth estate had arrived in force, creating an ambience of "all crisis, all the time." Twenty or more television crews lined two short blocks of Wall Street. The reporters were having trouble waylaying anybody of importance to interview. Most of the Street's true powers, the people Tom Wolfe had named "the giants of the earth," were either using alleys and rear entrances to avoid the reporters, or brushing past them, avoiding eye contact.

According to the "Style" section of the *Times*, most of the Wall Street grandees had only recently returned from the Hamptons or Nantucket. But they did not look fresh, energized, or even particularly powerful. The few possibly important figures that Edwin, Candy, and the television crews spotted looked frazzled. The September humidity, and the stress levels in their brokerages, investment banks, and law firms, were taking a severe toll on their two–thousand dollar suits and four–hundred dollar hairstyles.

On September 16, the Street's "giants" wanted to avoid conversations with CNBC "Money Honey" Maria Bartisimo, and the "Street Sweetie," Erin Burnett. Nobody wanted to provide sound bites for "Squawk on the Street." Today, the giants of the earth were determined to avoid allowing CNN's Lou Dobbs or Fox's Neil Cavuto to glibly comment on their "gloom" or "fright."

As Candy and Edwin walked up Wall toward Broadway, a young man with a microphone approached them. "Sir, are you from out of town?"

"Shore am," Edwin said. He resisted the urge to ask who else but a tourist would be on Wall Street in shorts, sandals, and a University of South Carolina Gamecocks polo shirt. While Candy was more upscale in designer jeans and a green sleeveless blouse, nobody would pick her as a broker, banker, or lawyer either.

"Could we interview you two?" the reporter said, gesturing toward his crew.

"Well, shore," Edwin said. "What station do you boys work for?" Candy reached into her purse for a comb.

"We're from New York 1, a local 24–hour cable news channel." He raised his microphone to about a foot from their mouths. "Where are you two from?"

"Aiken. A little bitty town in South Carolina," Edwin said.

Candy chimed in, "We came up to see the sights. Like the Statue of Liberty and the Empire State Building? Tonight we're going to see *Mama Mia*, you know, on Broadway?" She affected the habit of many southern women, ending sentences with question marks. "And tomorrow morning we're going to Rockefeller Plaza to see the folks on the *Today* show, when they come outside? We've even made us a little 'Aiken, S.C.' sign."

The reporter got down to business. "Have you heard about the big trouble on Wall Street?"

Edwin held up his *New York Post*. "Indeed we have."

"President Bush said the economy of the United States is fundamentally sound," said New York 1. "Do you find that reassuring?" Edwin looked straight into the camera lens, assumed his most portentous classroom manner, and said, "That's exactly what President Hoover said back in 1929. And of course it wasn't true. But it was probably the right thing to say. Proclaiming that the economy was collapsing would only have spread the panic faster and made things even worse." He added some gratuitous comments about Hoover being a true tragic figure. "Did you know he lived out his last years right here, in the Waldorf Astoria?"

New York 1 turned to Candy, "What about you, Ma'am?"

"I told my Sunday school class back in Aiken that the rich would have to pay for their sins, 'for it is easier for a camel to pass through the eye of a needle than for a rich man to enter the Kingdom of Heaven,' the Bible says."

The reporter must have decided that he had found some comic relief on a grim day. "Does this financial trouble cause you to think about visiting New York? Will you be more cautious about how much you spend while you are here?"

"We're pretty careful anyhow," Edwin said.

"You won't find us eating at Elaine's or the Russian Tea Room," Candy said. "TGI Friday or the Red Lobster are plenty good enough for our 35ᵗʰ wedding anniversary tomorrow night. Did you know that the world's largest TGI Friday's is right here in New York, on Times Square? No reservations required?"

The reporter saw he had recorded well beyond thirty seconds. "I hope you two will enjoy your anniversary celebration, and the rest of your visit. This is Lewis Frazier, New York 1, reporting from Wall Street."

"Do you think your station will use this?" Edwin said after the reporter shut down.

"Oh yes. If you can get back to your hotel room, it should be on in about thirty minutes. We'll probably show it three or four times."

Edwin and Candy headed across Broadway; Candy held her laughter down to a snicker until they reached the foot of the steps up to Trinity Church. She snorted and said, "You old goat! Lecturing a twenty–year–old about Herbert

312

Hoover! That kid has never even *heard* of President Hoover. He probably hasn't heard of Richard Nixon."

Edwin collapsed against the wall at the base of the churchyard. "Red Lobster! Our anniversary at TGI Friday's!" He slapped at the stairway wall. "Your Sunday School class?"

Candy, held both hands over her abdomen and shrieked, "Why SHORE!"

Even on a bad day, it is possible to have fun in the financial district.

About the Author

Von Pittman has had the honor and pleasure of administering programs and teaching in the distance education units of four first–rate state universities.

He has collected many prizes and awards for his writing, and his fiction and nonfiction has been published in many anthologies, magazines, and other publications dating from his working days to the present. Von is now retired and lives in Mid–Missouri.

CPSIA information can be obtained
at www.ICGtesting.com
Printed in the USA
FFHW021544070819
54141835-59836FF